31

THE GIRLS OF CANBY HALL

HERE COMES THE BRIDESMAID

EMILY CHASE

SCHOLASTIC INC.
New York Toronto London Auckland Sydney

—for Wilhelmina Martin Eaken
and Dorothy Campbell Bump
even though it wasn't a boarding school

ISBN 0-590-41673-1
Copyright © 1988 by B.B. Hiller All rights reserved. Pub-
lished by Scholastic Inc.

THE GIRLS OF CANBY HALL is a registered trademark
of Scholastic Inc.

12 11 10 9 8 7 6 5 4 3 2 1   8 9/8 0 1 2 3/9

Printed in the U.S.A.   01

First Scholastic printing, December 1988

31

THE GIRLS OF CANBY HALL

HERE COMES THE BRIDESMAID

THE GIRLS
OF CANBY HALL

CHAPTER ONE

"I'm bored," Jane Barrett announced to her roommates, fellow students at Canby Hall. Jane was lying on top of clumps of clothes scattered on her unmade bed. She stared at the ceiling as if there might be an answer to her plight written on it.

Andrea Cord stood up from her desk, abandoning her algebra, to tend to her friend. She reached for Jane's wrist and pretended she was checking her pulse. She swept a hand gently across Jane's forehead.

"Is it serious?" October Houston asked in mock concern.

"It's a serious case of the mid-semester blues," Andy told them grimly. "And, I think it's catching."

"Because absolutely nothing interesting is going on," Jane said, pulling herself up to a sitting position. "Not even exams!"

"Now, I *know* it's serious," Toby said.

1

"When Jane starts thinking there's something good to be said about exams, we're in trouble! Quick, think of something interesting that's been happening around here."

`"Well, I've been working hard on my dance solo," Andy reminded the girls. Andy's dream was to dance with a national troupe, preferably as a soloist. She often spent lonely but happy hours in Canby Hall's auditorium with classical or contemporary music blasting from a cassette player, leaping and pirouetting.

"That's fine for *you*," Jane told her. "But there isn't anything interesting going on for Toby and me."

Toby squinted her eyes and regarded her roommates carefully. They were about as different as three people could be. Redheaded October Houston, Toby for short, was the daughter of a Texas ranch owner. Her mother had died when Toby was very young. Toby had been raised in the lonely range country, where a girl's best friend was her horse, in Toby's case one named Max.

Jane, on the other hand, came from a long line of socialite Bostonians with loads of money, and with her smooth, long, blonde hair and impeccable clothes, she looked the part. Canby Hall even had a building named after the Barrett family. And there was a Barrett wing of the art museum in Boston, and a Barrett Settlement House in a poor section of the city. Toby and Andy sometimes teased Jane that the Barretts were probably being served crumpets at the Boston Tea Party — by the rebels, of course. Jane never denied the possibility.

Andy, from Chicago, came from a large and loving black family that owned a restaurant, where everybody (once even roommates) pitched in. There was so much love in the Cord family that sometimes it almost seemed too much — except when the Care Packages arrived. Andy's mother was a wonderful cook and the girls couldn't decide which goody they liked best — the caramel corn, the brownies, the chocolate chip cookies, the sponge cake with strawberry filling, the chocolate drops, or the homemade turtles. And, just when they thought they'd decided, another package would arrive with something even *better*.

But on a cold, gray day in the middle of the semester, even a Care Package couldn't bring an enthusiastic response from Jane.

"I'm bored," she repeated.

"Come on, Toby, Jane's relying on us to remind her of the really fun things that are coming up that she can look forward to."

"Midterms," Toby suggested.

Jane tossed a pillow at her. "*Fun*, I said. Even interesting will do. Midterms don't fit either description."

"Eleanor Masters was all excited about

something yesterday," Toby said. "Don't know what it was, though."

"I do," Jane said. "She got a stamp from Sri Lanka for her collection."

"Be still my heart!" Andy said. "Sri Lanka? Wow!"

Jane gave her a withering look.

"Not good enough for you, huh?" Andy asked.

Jane shook her head.

Toby glanced out the window at the ancient oaks which covered the campus — their leaves now gold and red in the dappled sunshine of the afternoon.

"The annual leaf-raking is just around the corner," Toby told them.

Both girls glared at Toby. She shrugged. Canby Hall was an old school located in a small town in Massachusetts. It had been founded in memory of Julia Canby, and the girls joked that she must have had a *lot* of memories because the school had an awful lot of traditions that the school's headmistress, Patrice Allardyce (called P.A., behind her back), insisted dated back to Julia's own childhood. Among the traditions was Leaf-raking Day — not high on the student's list of favorites.

"Swell, I can look forward to chillblains and blisters," Jane said.

"I don't think you're getting into the spirit here," Andy told her.

"I know something else that's coming up,"

Toby drawled in her Texas twang. "It's that essay contest that P.A. was telling us about at the assembly Monday."

"Oh, right: 'The Most Interesting Person I've Ever Met,' " Andy said.

Jane yawned. "And I suppose you'll do an essay about Eleanor and her stamp collection," she suggested.

"Oh, come on, Jane," Andy said, a little annoyed. "Stamp collecting can be fascinating."

Andy had a way of finding the bright side of almost everything, but Jane thought she was stretching it in this case.

"Stamp collecting *may* be interesting," Jane conceded finally. "But Eleanor definitely is not."

"I can't argue with you on that one," Andy agreed. "Actually, though, I was thinking of writing about Allegra for the essay contest."

"Hey, that's a neat idea," Jane said, suddenly not so bored. "She *is* interesting." Jane swung her legs over the edge of her bed and leaned forward. "I kind of miss her, too, don't you?"

"Oh, yes," Andy said.

"In a way," Toby added.

Allegra was Princess Allegra of Montavia — a small principality in central Europe. Allegra had spent a week on the Canby Hall campus the previous year, hoping to be able to go to school there. As it turned out, though, she'd had to return to her home. But before she'd gone, she'd left a very strong impression on the whole school — especially on the three girls in Room 407 of Baker House.

Allegra had surprised them. She had not fit their image of a princess at all. She'd become a good friend, although one with special problems. After all, her whole life had been planned for her, including an arranged marriage. Some of the plans had even been made before she'd been born. What Allegra had wanted from Canby Hall was to be treated just like the other girls of Canby Hall — not as a special person. It had almost worked, too, until she'd fallen in love. When Allegra and Randy Crowell — a handsome local boy who lived on a nearby horse farm — fell for each other, the princess had started playing hide-and-seek with her bodyguards, and ended up trying to run away from everybody and everything.

Finally, Allegra had realized that, much as she might want it, she *wasn't* like everybody else, and she did have to return to Montavia. And she had to forget about Randy.

While she'd been on the Canby campus, Allegra and Andy had become close friends, and they'd exchanged letters regularly since her return to Montavia. Allegra even called once because she'd wanted to tell Andy about a ballet she'd seen in Paris. Andy was enchanted by Allegra's description of the dance.

"Have you heard from her recently?" Jane asked.

"Nope," Andy said. "But the last time she wrote, she said she thought she was going to have some interesting news for me soon, so I've really been waiting for her next letter."

"You reminded me of something," Jane said. She began shuffling through a stack of papers she kept near her desk (she couldn't keep them on her desk because the desk itself was such a mess). "My mother sent me a clipping. It's here someplace, and I wanted to show it to you right away, but you were at the auditorium."

"Yesterday?" Andy asked.

"Oh, no, this was a couple of weeks ago."

"Barrett Pony Express," Toby joked. "We take the long cut."

Jane ignored Toby and continued her search. Papers began to slither onto the floor. "I know it's here someplace," Jane assured Toby and Andy. "It was about Allegra. It was in the Boston paper. Something about her and her fiancé at the opera in Paris, I think? It's right . . . here!" She produced a rumpled clipping.

"Let me see!" Andy said eagerly. She took the clipping and began reading out loud. "Says here 'The vivacious young lovers . . . ' Young *lovers*!" Andy hooted. "Why,

Frederick is thirty-five! And vivacious isn't the word Allegra used to describe him. Sounded like he's the kind of guy who would get excited about Eleanor's stamp from Sri Lanka."

"Read on, for goodness sake!" Toby urged her. "Save the editorial remarks for later."

"Okay, okay," Andy agreed. " 'The vivacious young lovers were seen sharing a private joke in the royal box at the opera.' Look, here's a picture, but it's kind of fuzzy."

The three girls pored over the photograph.

"Yep, that's Allegra!" Toby announced.

"Sure it's Allegra, but is it *Frederick*?" Andy asked.

"That doesn't look like the Frederick she described to us, at all," Jane agreed. "For one thing, he doesn't look thirty-five, for another, he doesn't look boring. In fact he looks rather, uh . . . " She searched for the word she wanted.

"Dashing?" Andy suggested.

"Handsome?" Toby offered.

Jane paused a moment to consider. "Actually, *cute* was what I was going to say."

They looked again. Cute was the word.

The girls sat down on their separate beds, puzzlement on their faces. Jane clutched the clipping in her hand, glancing at it from time to time. She shook her head.

"It's not Frederick," she concluded. Toby

and Andy nodded their heads in agreement.

"And it's not Randy Crowell, either," Toby observed to her friends.

"But she said she absolutely *had* to marry this guy, Frederick from Almare," Andy reminded her friends. "The whole deal was that after they get married, the two kingdoms would be united. They probably even had all kinds of summit meetings to decide whether it would be called Montavia or Almare or Monmare or Altavia, or something like that."

"Well, if it's not Frederick and it's not Randy, what *is* going on?" Andy asked.

"I can't wait until you get that next letter from Allegra. Sounds like she wasn't fooling when she told you she had some news for you!" Toby said. "This is *fun*," she added, grinning.

"And it's *not* boring," Jane declared emphatically.

CHAPTER TWO

The next afternoon, Andy slung her gym bag over her shoulders, reassuring herself that she'd remembered everything she needed for her dance practice. She had been dashing to the auditorium every afternoon after academic classes ended since she'd begun working on the *Romeo and Juliet* solo. It was the most exciting piece — and the most difficult — she'd ever done. And *so* romantic.

Andy could easily picture herself as Juliet, the star-crossed lover, hopelessly drawn to Romeo, the one man in the world she couldn't marry. The tragedy, the beauty, the drama, the romance — she loved every bit of it. In addition to loving the story, she also loved the music and the choreography. Andy thought it a stunning solo, one of the most challenging in the ballet, and certainly the hardest she had ever attempted.

Through hard work, Andy had been admitted to the advanced dance program. That meant that not only did she work with the other students on programs the class would perform, but that she was one of the selected dancers who would do a solo at the spring recital. It was many months away, but as far as Andy was concerned, it wasn't too soon to be perfecting her dance. After all, if she was good enough, one day she might, just might, do this very solo as part of a performance of the entire ballet in a professional troupe!

For now, that was just one of Andy's dreams.

"What's the faraway look in your eyes?" Jane asked, studying Andy as she paused before leaving Room 407.

"It's my future," Andy told her with confidence, and then wafted out the door, floating on her own dreams.

On her way out of the dorm, Andy barely paused at her mailbox. She pulled out a handful of envelopes and jammed them into her gym bag — next to two pairs of toe shoes, her leotard, tights, leg warmers, towels, and cassette player. Yes, she'd remembered everything.

Some practices went better than others. Andy knew that. That's how it was for a dancer. Some days your body could do everything the way you wanted it to, and some days it couldn't.

That day was one of the unsatisfying kind. She'd worked for two hours on a very small section of the solo involving a series of *jetés*, broad leaps with one leg stretched forward and the other back, sort of like splits in midair, across the stage, followed by *pirouettes* to return her to center stage, where the most moving part of the entire solo took place. Andy could do all the *jetés* and *pirouettes*. The trouble was that she couldn't do them in time to the music, which spoiled her good mechanics.

She was terribly discouraged by the time she got back to Room 407, and she felt doubly bad because her roommates were both deep into their studies. Andy hadn't meant to spend two hours at dance practice. She had an algebra assignment to work on that was giving her trouble. She knew she would have spent the time more productively on her toes about quadratic equations rather than on her toes *en pointe*.

She slammed her gym bag down on her bed, startling Toby and Jane into reluctantly acknowledging her presence. Andy, normally sunny, could be depressed by only one thing — failure at ballet. Jane and Toby knew better than to ask how her practice had gone.

Andy plopped onto her bed and began yanking her things out of her bag. It wasn't until she got to the bottom of the bag, to where her letters had migrated, that she had anything to smile about. For one of the letters had the now familiar postmark of Montavia.

"Hey, guys! Look at this! I got a letter from Allegra — in fact," she said, looking at another envelope from the bag, "I have *two*!"

"Hey, great! What does she say?" Jane demanded.

"I don't know yet," Andy said. "I'm going to have to read the letters first."

Toby crossed her arms in front of her. In anyone else, that would have been a sign of impatience, but in the laid-back Texas redhead, it meant she knew she had to wait. She waited.

Andy looked at each envelope carefully.

"What are you looking at? The stamps? You can give them to Eleanor later," Jane told her.

"No, I just wanted to see which letter was mailed first, so I read them in the right order," Andy explained.

Jane crossed her arms in front of her. In her, it was a sign of impatience.

Eventually, Andy figured out which letter to read first from the Montavian postmark.

"She's getting married!" Andy shrieked.

"Of course she is. We knew that already," Toby reminded Andy.

"But what we didn't know is that she's getting married in just, exactly" — Andy looked at the calendar which hung on their wall — "four weeks from today."

"Just four more weeks of freedom," Toby remarked, recalling how much Allegra was dreading her life as Frederick's wife.

"Then long nights of state dinners and days of cutting ribbons," Jane added.

"And years of boredom!" Andy commiserated.

The girls knew enough of the life of royalty to know that it wasn't all glamour and fun. Most of it was, in fact, dreadfully dull and repetitious ceremony. And it was clear from what Allegra had told them when she'd stayed at Baker House, too, that Allegra was definitely *not* looking forward to it.

"Say, what about that man she was with at the opera? Does she say anything about him? It must have been awfully embarrassing for Frederick when the newspapers thought it was him, don't you think?"

"She doesn't say anything about that," Andy said, hurriedly scanning the first letter. "But then, of course, she would have no way of knowing about the mistake in a Boston paper, would she?"

"No," the girls agreed.

"You going to read the next letter?" Toby asked. "Or are you going to let it ripen a bit, along with our curiosity?"

Andy blushed. "Right, yeah, the next letter. Okay, I'll read it out loud." She slit the envelope, carefully preserving the stamp for Eleanor.

There was a long silence. Jane waited as long as she could, watching Andy's face change from solemn concentration, to surprise, and then to joy.

"I can't stand it anymore!" Jane declared, annoyed. "*What* is going on?"

"It's the wedding," Andy mumbled.

"What *about* the wedding?" Jane persisted.

There was a long silence while Andy continued to read, flipping the rich vellum page over to read both sides.

"*Andy!*" Jane said in exasperation. "What about the wedding?"

Andy's eyes lit up as she looked at her two friends. "Well, for one thing," she began, so slowly and tantalizingly, that even Toby was sitting on the edge of her bed. "For one thing," she repeated, "we're all invited."

"Wow!" Jane said. "Wouldn't it be fabulous to go to a royal wedding? Can you imagine?"

"It sure was decent of her to think of us," Toby added. "Too bad it's the middle of the semester, and we won't be able to go. Think she'd consider putting the thing off a few months?"

"No way," Andy said. "And I'm not so sure we — or at least *I* — won't go."

"You think you might go?" Jane asked, frankly jealous of the very idea.

"Well, I'll have to consider it," Andy said. "After all," she paused for dramatic effect,

"I'm to be one of the bridesmaids!"

"You are?!" Jane and Toby yelped, practically in chorus.

Andy's grin told them that it was true. "Yep, she says she wants all three of us there, and she's fully prepared to have her father and mother make a Royal Proclamation that Canby Hall should spring us, and the royal family will pay our plane fare so that we can all be there. Isn't that wonderful?"

"Fabulous!" Jane answered, excitedly. "But" — suddenly her face fell — "you can't possibly go — not now."

"What do you mean?" Andy retorted.

"Well, when there's so much excitement going on on the campus — you know, leaf-raking, the Sri Lanka stamp. I mean, how could we consider abandoning Canby Hall in such a thrilling period of its existence?"

Andy tossed a pillow at Jane and looked at Toby for sympathy.

"What do you say, Toby? Will you come to Montavia with me?"

Toby shrugged. "I don't know, Andy," she said. "It's hard to imagine what it would be like. Why, I don't even know how to act with all those royal people. Everybody would be spending all their time telling me which fork to use, you know?"

"Oh, I don't think it would be that way at all," Andy assured her. "After all, before Allegra got here, remember how concerned we were about what she'd be like? Remember how we were afraid she'd be a snob? It turned out she was really just like us. . . . Well, there were a few differences," Andy conceded, when her roommates stared at her in disbelief.

"Right, like the fact that she was trailed by bodyguards, and was going to marry a prince and be a queen. . . ." Jane reminded her.

"Speaking of being a queen, though, Allegra said something about that in her letter." Andy reached for it and began skimming it over. "Here it is," she read, " 'And now that I've finally learned to be a princess, I think being a queen must be very different. You three are going to have to help me on this. Please.' "

"Us three?" Toby said in surprise. "What can she mean by that? How can we teach her something about being a queen? All I know anything about, really, is horseback riding, and she's as good as I am at that."

"All I know about is my family's restaurant — and my dancing, of course," Andy said.

"And all I know about is Boston. There are many women in Boston who *think* they are queens, but it's not remotely like the real thing. I mean, I always do well in history — "

"Maybe that's it," Andy said. "Allegra knows about all our studying. Maybe she's counting on us to let her know how queens and kings have acted through the ages."

"You mean like so she won't get deposed and beheaded like Marie Antoinette?" Toby asked ominously. "Allegra'll never say 'Let them eat cake.' "

"Do you want to give me a break?" Andy asked. "Allegra is nothing like Marie Antoinette, and I don't think Montavia is much like pre-revolutionary France. After all, these are *civilized* times — "

"But we're still going to have to do more studying if we're to be of any use to Allegra," Toby pointed out.

"More important than that, we're going to have to do some fast talking," Jane said.

Both girls looked at her.

"Well, there's the little matter of a lot of time off from school," she said. "And then there are passports, airfare, wardrobes, just a few tiny items. . . ."

"If Allegra needs us, we'll find a way to be there!" Andy pronounced stubbornly.

"And if she's actually going to marry drippy old Frederick, she's going to need us a *lot*," Jane said.

"Oh, didn't I tell you?" Andy said, suddenly surprised.

"Tell us what?" Toby responded.

"She's not marrying Frederick at all — "

"You mean she's not going to be the queen of the two kingdoms together?" Jane said, confused.

"Yes, she is that, but it's not by marrying Frederick. You see, it turned out that Frederick wasn't such a dullard. He fell in love with somebody who was totally unsuitable to be his wife and queen, but he refused to forsake her and marry Allegra, so the old boy has some spine after all. Anyway, he married this woman and has moved out of the country. He's given up the throne. 'Abdication' is what Allegra called his decision to leave. So, Allegra is to marry Frederick's brother James."

"He's probably just as fascinating as his older brother," Toby said.

"I don't think so. Here's what she wrote about him," Andy said, picking up Allegra's letter again. " 'You wouldn't believe James is actually Frederick's brother. He's simply wonderful, and he absolutely swept me off my feet. You should have seen us when we went to the opera in Paris! We had a wonderful time. He's so handsome and dashing. I know this is gushy, but I can't help myself.' " Andy paused significantly and then continued reading from Allegra's letter. " 'He's cute. I can't wait to marry him. You've just *got* to be here. All three of you! And Andy,' she writes, 'I want you to dance at my wedding.' Won't that be romantic?"

Andy looked back up at her friends. They each glanced at one another, almost too excited to speak. Jane broke the silence.

"First dibs on the phone!" she announced, dashing into the hall.

There was no doubt about it: The roommates would find a way, somehow, to get to Allegra's wedding. It was a once in a lifetime opportunity, and they weren't about to miss it because of a few minor obstacles.

CHAPTER THREE

It seemed like the next few weeks were the busiest in the girls' lives. There was a constant whirl of activity in Room 407.

At first, the activity consisted mostly of phone calls between Canby Hall and the girls' families. Jane's family was the easiest to convince. Toby teased her that royal weddings must be very commonplace to the Barretts.

Andy's family was thrilled for her and wanted her to go, but they were very uncomfortable with the idea that she'd be even *further* away from Chicago. What finally convinced them was when Andy explained that, not only was she to be a bridesmaid, but she was also going to give her first command performance for royalty. Andy's parents felt that it might be the opportunity Andy needed to demonstrate her ability to people who could help her. Andy didn't think that such help was likely, but since it was the deciding factor, she didn't want to set them straight.

For Toby, parental approval of the long trip to Montavia was a little more difficult. In the first place, she had a rough time getting hold of her father. He was working day and night to break in some new horse. Every time she got him on the phone, he was just dashing out to the corral again. She only got him to stay on the phone long enough to explain the situation when he thought she was telling him *she* was going to get married.

Eventually, the misunderstanding was cleared up, and Toby's father agreed to let her go. But he didn't seem to see anything so special about the royal wedding. After all, everybody knew that the most fun kind of wedding was when Parrish McCoy could call the square dances. Toby smiled when her dad told her that. They'd been to a lot of parties and weddings in Texas where Parrish McCoy had done the "calling." She had to agree that McCoy was the best. In fact, it was entirely possible that Allegra's wedding would be more fun if Parrish *could* be there. Somehow, though, she suspected that there wouldn't be any square dancing at Allegra's wedding.

"Well, Dad," she said. "You know how these royals are."

"Yep," he said. "And I guess you've got

to be there instead of reading about it in the paper, huh?"

"Yep," she said.

And so it was decided.

After the girls got their okays from their parents, the next big step was P.A. They knew that Ms. Allardyce would remember Allegra's visit to the Canby Hall campus *extremely* well — especially since it had nearly been a total disaster. The roommates decided that the only way to get her to permit them to take time off from school would be to show her that they knew how to act properly and that they had a purpose — not just to have fun.

It took them two days to decide just how to approach Ms. Allardyce — and they needed a lot of help from Meredith Pembroke, their housemother. Merry was one hundred percent behind them and made some terrific suggestions.

In the end, at Merry's suggestion, the girls invited the headmistress for tea at Merry's apartment on the top floor of Baker House. Ms. Allardyce's idea of a proper gathering always seemed to involve tea. When one was summoned to Ms. Allardyce's house, tea was served. The girls did everything just right, polishing the teapot until it gleamed and putting out the most elegant cookies and tea cake they could buy in town. But the setting would probably not have worked if Merry hadn't come up with the perfect suggestion to show Ms. Allardyce that they were serious.

When the headmistress was seated, starched napkin on her lap, cup balanced properly in one hand with a tea cake on the plate in front of her, the girls knew it was time to move into action. But nobody was quite sure how to start.

Typically, it was Andy who dived right in.

"Ms. Allardyce," she began, with a pleasant smile on her face, although she was so nervous that when she began speaking, it all came out in one very long jumbled sentence. "We're glad to welcome you to Baker House won't you have another tea cake and you remember Princess Allegra of Montavia well she's getting married and we're all invited to her wedding I'm even going to be a bridesmaid I mean I'm going to be one if you'll let us go our parents have said it's okay but we don't think it's going to be all just a lot of fun parties and we think we can learn something about government so if you'll let us go we'll do a project for you something like well Monarchy in the Modern World?"

At first, Jane and Toby just stared at Andy in total amazement. Then, without meaning to, but because Andy's speech had been much too funny to avoid it, Jane starting laughing. She'd never heard such a jumble of words and thoughts stream out of anybody's mouth at once in her life. Andy was horrified at Jane's laughter, but then she looked at Toby and saw that *her* shoulders were shaking, a sure sign that she was stifling giggles and was about to explode.

Andy thought it would be very handy if she could just die right then and there. She realized that she'd made a total nerd of herself — and in front of Ms. Allardyce! She looked at Merry for support, but Merry was looking down at her shoes with deeper concentration than Andy had noticed her give anything, and so Andy knew Merry wanted to laugh as well. Finally, Andy's eyes rested on Ms. Allardyce.

There was a long silence, punctuated only by Jane's stifled laughter and Toby's shaking. Merry shifted her feet and kept staring at her shoes.

Patrice Allardyce took a deep breath. Here it comes, Andy said to herself, prepared for the worst. She knew her friends were going to stop laughing soon and be very upset with her for wrecking their chances to go to the royal wedding.

"Well, girls," Ms. Allardyce began. "It seems that there are strings attached to this invitation to tea." She took a sip of her tea and a small bite of the tea cake. "I must confess that I have always admired a well-executed ulterior motive. I believe this party has several." She dabbed the corners of her mouth daintily with her napkin. "Naturally, I knew of Princess Allegra's wedding plans from the newspapers. It has, for example, been announced that one of the bridesmaids will be from America. I wondered if that might be you, Andrea. This tea party's agenda is not as much of a surprise to me as you may have expected."

Ms. Allardyce refilled her teacup while the girls stopped breathing, giggles subdued. They studied Ms. Allardyce intently. After the headmistress stirred her cup and replaced the spoon on the saucer, she sat back in her chair. The girls watched the steam spiral up off the top of the teacup.

"I think you have shown me several things today — first, that you care very much about this wedding and about your friendship with Her Royal Highness, Princess Allegra. Second, that you know how to prepare and, for the most part, act at a formal party." She focused on Jane so Jane would know that giggling was *not* part of acceptable behavior at a formal party. "And you have shown me that you have some purpose with your proposal to turn what might be viewed as a mere social event into a project for school."

She took a sip of her tea silently and then set the cup back onto her saucer with the faint click of porcelain on porcelain.

"You may go to Princess Allegra's wedding. Between now and your departure, you will each work ahead in your classes and on your assignments. Your teachers will give you extra time if you need it. You *will* do a joint project on Monarchy in the Modern World. You can hand it in to me within two weeks of your return. Is that all?"

"Yes, ma'am," Jane said, speaking for all of them.

"Then, I thank you for a lovely time. The tea was just right and the cakes were delicious, but I'm afraid I must be going now." With that, Ms. Allardyce stood up, nodded thanks and farewell to all of them, and left the room, moving as she always did, with a calm assurance and poise that made them think she'd been practicing it for years.

Ms. Allardyce reappeared in the door while the roommates were still holding their breath. "Bon voyage," their headmistress said with a smile, turned on her heel, and left.

"Yahoo!" Toby yowled as Ms. Allardyce's footsteps echoed down the hallway.

"We can go!" Andy joined in, jumping up out of her chair.

"It's off to the royal wedding! Fan-tastic!" Jane exclaimed.

Once they had Ms. Allardyce's permission as well as that of their parents, the job had only just begun. Not only did they have to work especially hard in all of their classes, but they had to get passports, and the biggest task of all, decide on their wardrobes.

"Imagine!" Jane gasped. "Four formal state dinners — *and* the wedding breakfast. I can't decide what to wear!"

"No problem for me," Toby said, shrugging. "I've just got the one yellow formal that I wore at the spring dance last year. It'll have to do."

"You can't wear the same dress four nights in a row!" Jane declared.

"Well, then, how about my jeans?" Toby retorted.

"I'm sorry," Jane said, quickly, realizing she'd hurt Toby's feelings. "I just meant that we are going to have to do some creative borrowing. You know, I have a blue silk dress that I think would look wonderful on you and Dee is about your size. . . ."

When the girls from Room 407 put out an emergency call for formal dresses, everybody in the school emptied out their closets. The students at Canby felt it was their personal responsibility to have Jane, Toby, and Andy be as well dressed as possible. Besides, everybody wanted to own a dress they could say had been worn at a royal wedding.

The biggest problem, it turned out, was the bridesmaid's dress for Andy. The royal major domo was *supposed* to send it to her for a fitting, but he ended up sending it to the wrong address. For a couple of days, it seemed like the dress would never arrive, but eventually, another one was dispatched.

"I hope he doesn't get sent into the dungeon for his mistake," Andy said, truly worried.

"I don't think that Monarchies in the Modern World do too much with dungeons these days," Jane suggested. "But if they do, then Allegra is right that she needs lessons in queening from us."

Andy was in Room 407, trying to figure out how to open the impossibly large box Allegra's dressmaker had sent her. Curiosity had brought in five other girls who lived on the fourth floor of Baker House. They watched in awe while Andy worked on the box.

"Dungeons! Give me a break! I thought we all got rid of all of those foolish preconceptions about royalty when we got to know Allegra last year. I mean, after all, people who are born into royal families are people just like *us* — except they chose their parents more carefully!"

Andy took her letter opener and slit along the brown paper tape which sealed the box. Andy's audience sat on the beds, chairs, and floor of the room and watched eagerly, laughing at Andy's joke.

"People are people. We know that, don't we?" Andy asked. Everybody nodded solemnly. Andy lifted the top off the box and continued her monologue. "There's nothing about any one person that makes them any better or any worse than any other person. For centuries people have been thinking about royalty as sort of magical fairy godpeople, but that's a lot of nonsense."

She drew away the yards of white tissue to reveal her bridesmaid's dress. It was all she could do to keep from gasping. Her classmates peered into the box eagerly.

The dress was bright pink watered silk. She held it up in front of her. The elegant lines of the dress began at the tight-fitting bodice with ruffled cap sleeves. The skirt flowed softly to the floor, a little wider at the hips, with a short train in the back.

While Andy chatted about how normal royal people really were, she slipped out of her jeans and sweatshirt top and into the pink dress.

"See, just by knowing Allegra as a friend, we know that there aren't any fairy godpeople, right?" she asked, and then waited for an answer from her friends while Toby did up the fabric-covered buttons which closed the gown in the back and Jane smoothed the skirt.

Jane and Toby stood back to get the full effect of the dress.

"She's wrong, you know," Jane said to Toby. Toby grinned in acknowledgement.

"About what?" Andy demanded.

"About the fairy godpeople," Jane explained. "Because if you go look in the mirror right now, I think you'll see that you're one of them."

Carefully, so as not to step on the hem of the floor-length gown, Andy made her way to the mirror hung on the back of her closet door.

"Oh!" she said in surprise, because there, standing in the mirror, was the closest thing she'd ever seen to a fairy godperson in her whole life. "I didn't know — " she uttered, nearly breathless with surprise at how different, and beautiful, she looked in the dress.

"Here comes the bridesmaid!" Toby announced and everybody began applauding.

CHAPTER FOUR

I don't believe this," Andy said a few days later when the girls were on the train from Amsterdam to Montavia. "Pinch me, and see if it's for real."

"Why would you want me to pinch you?" Toby asked, looking away from the train's window. "It's much more fun to look out the window than pinch."

"Well, sure, but it's all like something out of a storybook," Andy said. "Those mountains, for instance. . . ."

The girls had been met at their plane in Amsterdam by a Montavian diplomat who had escorted them to the train for the four-hour trip to Montavia's capital.

"It's hard to keep looking at the gorgeous mountains when somebody knocks on the door of our compartment every ten minutes or so to see if there's anything we need," Jane mused.

"I think I could get used to this," Toby told her. "I'm already getting to like being spoiled."

"That's the word exactly," Jane said. "I like it, too."

"But you've always *been* spoiled," Andy said.

"And I've always liked it," Jane told her matter-of-factly. Toby and Andy laughed.

There was a knock at their compartment door. A young man wearing a showy uniform entered. "Is there anything the young ladies would like at this time?" he asked.

"No, thank you," they told him. He bowed slightly and disappeared as discreetly as he'd appeared.

"We have to start considering how it is that we can help Allegra learn to be a queen," Andy said.

"Better question is why she apparently expects *us* to be able to do it," Toby said, stretching out her long, jean-clad legs, her feet propped up on the rich crushed velour seat which faced hers.

"The *why* isn't important," Andy told her friends. "It's almost like a royal decree, you know, so we'd better work on what we can do for her."

"Well, I brought my history book," Jane said. "Maybe she hasn't studied enough, so I've been looking up what all the good kings and queens in history have done."

"And?" Toby said expectantly.

"It's a little hard to tell because it's hard to find many monarchs who were completely good. Back in the old days, the first thing a new monarch did if he or she wanted to get off on the right foot with the peasants was to drain the swamps."

"Drain the swamps?" Andy said, incredulously.

"Sure, it creates more grazing land."

"Okay, so that's number one," Andy said, jotting it down on a fresh pad of paper which she'd hauled out of her overstuffed purse. "What do they do next?"

"Depends on who you think was good," Jane said. "Somebody like Queen Victoria of England was so influential — and lived so long — that a whole era was named after her, and it was a global influence."

"Ah, I can see it now," Andy said. " 'The Allegran Era,' " she grinned at her friends.

"Not if it means what the Victorian Era meant," Jane said darkly. "Victoria was this incredibly stiff person, and the Victorian era is mostly known for bigotry and prudishness in society and really ugly, uncomfortable furniture. Oh, and let's not forget about the social injustices of the late Industrial Revolution."

"I knew we shouldn't have let her take Modern European History," Andy groaned.

"So, what about Elizabeth the First — the redhead?" Toby asked.

"Oh," Jane smiled. "She was quite a ruler.

She ruled the country with an iron hand and established the British Empire. The whole palace was full of political intrigue, treason, and the like. And if she found out someone was plotting against her, heads rolled. I meant that quite literally, of course. Remember Mary Queen of Scots."

Toby and Andy nodded. They remembered quite well that Elizabeth had had her rival executed when she'd tried to usurp Elizabeth.

"Wasn't Shakespeare writing in those days? I mean, the Elizabethans were a pretty lively crew, weren't they?" Toby reminded Jane.

"That's true. Shakespeare was a genius and Elizabeth supported him and his troupe. He wrote dozens of plays. Some of them were performed at court. His history plays are particularly interesting because though there are usually lots of ways to interpret historical events, in his plays, Shakespeare always interpreted those events to please Elizabeth."

"Hmmm," said Andy, jotting down further notes.

"Allegra's got her work cut out for her, hasn't she?" Toby asked. Her friends agreed.

"And it's a little hard to see how we're going to help," Andy said, glancing down at the page she'd filled. "But we'll try."

"Maybe she wants us to help her from

our own experiences," Jane suggested. "After all, I've learned a lot about society from my own upbringing. I can teach her which fork to use and how to curtsey."

"Jane!" Andy said. "She already knows which fork to use — and the world will be curtseying to *her*, not the other way around."

The girls looked at Toby for a contribution. She lifted her eyebrows and dropped them again in resignation. "Look, the only thing I know anything about that the whole world doesn't also know is how to ride a horse, and run a ranch, and how to square dance. Allegra is as good on a horse as I am — maybe better, though I doubt she can rope a calf — and I don't figure she'll care much about ranching or square dancing anyway. Your turn, Andy. What can you teach her?"

"I wish I could teach her ballet, but I'm not good enough at it to teach — yet. I'm only good enough to dream. The only other thing I could teach her is waitressing. Mom and Dad would probably give her a job. For that, she's going to have to learn to hold the tray real high on her left hand, and prop it for balance with her shoulder and her right hand — then she can swing it around to put it on the caddy. . . ."

Jane and Toby started hooting. The image of Allegra being a waitress in the Cord family's restaurant was just too much.

"And what if she forgot that somebody

didn't want gravy?" Jane asked, laughing. "I can see the customers now: 'Your Royal Highness, scrap the gravy!' "

"Speaking of seeing," Toby said. "There's stuff to see now out the window. Let's look and not talk for a bit."

The track was cut into the mountainside, circling the snow-covered peaks, carrying the train up, over, and through the passes. The day was crystal clear, and they could see for miles. Villages were tucked into the valleys, probably looking much the same way they had hundreds of years ago. The houses had tiled roofs and the barns were often thatch-roofed.

"It's almost as if time had stopped here," Andy said, and her friends nodded.

The names of unfamiliar towns appeared on pillars at small stations where the train sometimes stopped. Only the reassuring reappearance of their personal attendant ("Is there anything I can get for you ladies?") told them that they were going to the right place.

Eventually, their attendant appeared with a coat over his uniform.

"We will be entering Montavia in ten minutes," he informed them. "Your suitcases will be removed for you and placed in the royal wagon." Discreetly, he backed out of the door, bowing ever so slightly as he went.

"Royal wagon!" Andy said, delight in her

voice, as she stuffed her papers, books, and magazines into her carryall. "Think that means we'll be in a horsedrawn stagewagon thing, all covered with gold filigree stuff just like Princess Di's wedding day?"

The girls jammed themselves up to the window so they could be the first to see Montavia. They could see snow-covered fields, but instead of the farmhouses and barns they'd noticed in the countryside, Montavia had large houses set into the mountainsides, allowing the inhabitants spectacular panoramic views.

"I think I'm going to like this place," Jane said.

"Me, too," Andy agreed, "especially when we get to ride through the streets in the royal wagon."

"Not bad," Toby admitted. "Not bad at all. But it's real rough grazing land for horses — too hilly." She began putting on her warm overcoat. The others did the same.

The train slowed down gently, finally stopping at a very small station with a single sign which read M NT VIA.

Their attendant opened the door for them and helped the girls step down from the train. Their bags were on the platform in front of them.

The girls stood, immobile for a few minutes, looking around, breathing the fresh mountain air deeply.

"So this is Montavia," Andy said finally.

"This way, ladies," the attendant told them politely, picking up all three large suitcases at once.

"But where's the royal wagon?" Jane asked her friends, not seeing anything with even the smallest touch of gold filligree.

"And the four horses to draw it?" Toby added.

"Just follow that man," Andy advised wisely. He threaded them through the small station house, where their passports were stamped and their suitcases were tagged for the palace. It only took a few seconds. They re-emerged into the sunlight into an ordinary parking lot. There was a single station wagon there with a driver at the wheel.

Their attendant walked directly to the rear of the station wagon, opened the back, and hefted their suitcases in.

"Oh," Jane said, barely masking her surprise. "The royal *station* wagon!" She started laughing.

Andy and Toby began laughing with her.

"I have the funny feeling that we're in for a couple of surprises over the next few days," Andy said.

"I think you're right about that," Jane said.

"Yep," Toby agreed.

They climbed into the backseat of the spacious station wagon ("Nine-passenger," Jane pointed out to them).

"I can't wait to see Allegra," Jane said.

"Yeah, and tell her what we thought the royal wagon was going to be," Andy added. "She's going to think that's as funny as we do."

It was very comforting to know that in this strange land, with strange customs, not only would they be able to share things with one another, but they had a friend who lived there who would understand as well.

CHAPTER FIVE

"Andy!" The familiar voice of Princess Allegra rang out across the courtyard. The three girls were just climbing out of the royal wagon when Allegra spotted them from a second-floor window. "Hi! Hello, Jane and Toby, too!" She waved energetically.

The roommates waved back at her.

"Come on up!" Allegra called. "I'm waiting for you in your suite."

"Our *suite!*" Toby said, eyes opening wide.

"We'll be right there," Andy called to Allegra, trying to herd her friends toward the door. But there was work to do first. Somehow, during all the hours they'd traveled, by plane, train, and royal wagon, their belongings seemed to have scattered. Even the backseat of the station wagon was cluttered with magazines and half-empty candy boxes. With Andy directing traffic

("Get the wrapper. Jane, can you reach my knitting?"), they were soon following their chauffeur, whose name they had learned was Fenster. It wasn't clear whether it was Mr. Fenster or Fenster something, so they just called him Fenster. Fenster led them through the grand entrance gate of the palace, home of the King and Queen of Montavia.

"Get this!" Jane hissed, out of Fenster's earshot, pointing to the portcullis suspended above the castle entryway. It was an iron gate designed to slam down before or on advancing enemies. Then, just inside the castle entry, stood a group of mannequins garbed in medieval armor. "I guess Allegra's forebears were serious about defense."

"This place is like a museum," Andy remarked in a whisper as she walked along the hallway, staring at the artwork that included tapestries on the walls. "It's just exactly what I was expecting."

"Why are you whispering?" Toby asked her friends.

Andy seemed to be surprised to learn that she *had* been whispering. Jane had the answer. "We're whispering because we feel like we're in a museum, and if we talk too loud, the guard is going to tell us to be quiet." She glanced at Fenster, but he didn't seem to want to tell them anything at all. He walked slowly and steadily, seemingly unbothered by the burden of their suitcases.

For a few minutes, the girls were quiet, following Fenster. It seemed that the whole downstairs of the palace was a series of gigantic rooms, and everywhere they looked, there were signs of royal preparations for a royal wedding — unless this was everyday life for royalty. One particularly large room had a wooden floor which was being polished and buffed by eight people at once. In another room, preparations were being made for a feast. There was no food, but table after table had been laid with elegant china, crystal, and silver. Even Jane gasped at the sight.

Fenster then turned to the left and led them up a sweeping staircase, lit by streams of sunlight coming through the stained glass windows. He turned right at the top of the stairs and continued walking.

"We should be leaving a trail of papers behind us," Andy said. "Otherwise, we'll never find our way back."

"Oh, sure we will," Toby assured her. "I remember clearly: It's along the hall past the ballroom, through the conservatory, library on the left, billiard room on the right — "

"Where Miss Peacock killed Colonel Mustard with the lead pipe?" Andy suggested.

"You got it," Toby replied, grinning mischievously.

At that moment, Fenster came to such a

sudden halt in a doorway that Andy nearly bumped into him. He bowed deeply from his waist.

"Your Royal Highness," he said.

"It's all right, Fenster," Allegra said from within the room. "Let them in."

Still bowing, or perhaps leaning forward because the suitcases were getting so heavy after such a long walk from the front door, Fenster stepped aside to allow the girls into the room. There was Allegra, waiting for them. In spite of the gigantic castle with its oversized rooms, spectacular art, portcullis, armor, and rooms full of servants readying the whole place for her royal wedding, Allegra was just Allegra, the same person they remembered so well and so fondly from her visit to Canby Hall.

"Hey, you look great!" Andy said. The three roommates stood in a row at the door to the suite, taking it all in.

"Me? You're the ones who look wonderful. I'm so glad you're here. I was afraid that something was going to go wrong — that Ms. Allardyce wouldn't let you come, and I really didn't want to get married without you here." She stood in the middle of a large pink and gold room, grinning broadly. Finally, she put her arms out, inviting them all to come for a hug. "Welcome to Montavia!" she told them.

They ran past a rather tired Fenster to give the bride-to-be her royal hug.

"Is this place really for us?" Toby asked. "Or is this where all the partying is going to take place?" She was poking around the suite and couldn't believe what she saw. "Why, I've seen ranges with entire herds of cattle that aren't as big as this place!"

Jane and Andy gaped at Toby for a minute, but when they saw the twinkle in her eye, they knew she was just joking. Besides, the place *was* huge.

"Go on, take a look," Allegra invited.

The suite consisted of two very large rooms — a sitting room and a sleeping room — plus a bathroom.

"The bathroom alone is as big as good old Room 407 in Baker House," Andy remarked.

"Well, if it'll make you more comfortable to sleep in the bathtub, you may," Allegra teased. "But since all of you were so nice about fixing up a special room for me when I came to Canby Hall, I thought it was the least I could do for you here."

Both the sitting room and the bedroom were decorated with elaborate ornate furniture, obviously antiques. In the bedroom, Allegra had managed to have all three beds placed around the room in the same configuration which the girls had in Room 407.

"Just like home," Jane sighed, plopping herself onto her bed.

"Hey, look at this!" Toby said, delighted. The girls turned to see what had her so excited. There, on the ceiling, fourteen feet above the floor, hung a tea bag, which had been taped to the ceiling. "How'd you manage that?" she asked, grinning.

"I remembered that you had such a thing in Room 407," Allegra explained. "I don't know why it's there, but it's there and I assume it's important to you, so I had Fenster put it on the ceiling for you. English Breakfast Tea — is that okay?"

"Mostly, I just have plain old tea, but English Breakfast will be fine while I'm here. It's a little upscale, of course, but so's this whole place."

"This is just wonderful, Allegra," Jane told her as she began unpacking her suitcase. Jane's idea of unpacking was to open the case and dump all her clothes on her bed. Allegra smiled. "If you'll wait, there'll be someone along to do your unpacking shortly."

"Oh. Great . . . We're glad to be here. Now, if we can just get through your royal wedding without doing anything terribly un-royal. P.A. has told us that we're not only representing Canby Hall, but also the whole of the United States of America, and we don't want to embarrass all those people we're representing." As Jane finished speaking, a woman appeared in the door, nodded pleasantly to everyone, and began to unpack and hang up and put away everyone's clothes.

"All you have to do is be yourselves," Allegra assured the girls.

While the unpacking continued, the girls chatted. What they were mostly interested in was Prince James, and Allegra had a lot to say about him.

"I can't tell you how lucky I am," she said. "He's absolutely everything his brother Frederick wasn't. Of course, he's older than I am, but he's not *old* if you know what I mean. I'm *so* lucky," she said, squeezing herself with her own arms, happiness sparkling from her. "Not only am I in love, and it's like it never was before," she gave the girls a knowing look to remind them that she'd thought she was in love with Randy Crowell when she'd been at Canby Hall, "but even more importantly, I have a friend — a best friend — a friend for life. All I can say is that when the time comes for you all to marry, I hope you're as lucky as I am."

"Get married?" said Toby. "Maybe. But I'll have a ranch to run. That comes first!"

Andy smiled. "I don't know, either," she confessed. "I'm happy for you, for sure, but I can't see myself getting married for a long time, if ever. If I do, it sure won't be until I'm finished school and college and my first few years of professional dancing, and — "

"Sounds like you don't want to get married until you're an old lady!" Jane teased.

"Well, twenty-two at least," Andy asserted. Suddenly, it occurred to her that she had a *friend* who was getting married, to say nothing of taking on the governing of a whole — if smallish — country. Having a crush on somebody or even thinking you were in love with somebody was one thing, but marriage? The realization of it all made her shiver. "Isn't it scary for you to be marrying so young?" she asked Allegra finally.

"A little," Allegra confessed, "but then remember, I'm older than you are. It's easy to forget because we got to be such good friends, but I'll be twenty next month. That's probably *still* too young for most people to get married, but then *most* people aren't marrying James."

No matter how wonderful James was, when she thought about it, Andy was more than a little glad it was Allegra who was getting married and not herself. Her commitment was to ballet, not romance.

When all of Andy's things had been put away, the girls were ready to have some fun. They walked back into their sitting room. Allegra showed them how to ring for Fenster. When he arrived, she asked him to bring them some sodas and a snack. Almost before they could get comfortable, the goodies appeared.

"Not as good as your mother's," Allegra said, munching happily on a cookie.

Everybody in the world knew that Andy's

parents' Care Packages were the best in the school.

"I'll tell my mom that," Andy promised. "She'll be pleased to know." At the same time, Andy promised herself that she was going to start keeping a diary of this trip. There were too many unbelievable things happening, and she didn't want to forget one of them, especially that the Princess of Montavia remembered how good her mother's cooking was.

"So how is it we're supposed to help you with being a queen?" Toby asked typically bluntly.

"Any way you can!" Allegra said. "My mother is so involved with the wedding that she's nearly useless."

Andy and Toby looked to Jane to begin.

"She's the best history student," Andy explained, nodding toward Jane. Allegra looked at Jane expectantly.

Jane took a deep breath. "Well," she began. "We've been doing some studying on queens in history, and we've come up with a list of dos and don'ts, but we're not sure they're exactly what you want — "

"Anything," Allegra said. "Just tell me how to be a good queen. I know I can count on you!"

"All right," Jane said, sitting up straight. "First thing you do is to drain the swamps."

The girls looked at Allegra for her reaction. At first, the princess's face was solemn. Then she sort of hunched forward and suddenly exploded into uncontrollable laughter.

The roommates didn't know what to do, but then it was so clear that the look on Allegra's face was complete joyful hysteria that they started laughing, too.

Eventually, Allegra's giggles slowed down enough for her to talk. "I knew," she said, "that I was right that I needed you three here with me."

"Well, what's so funny about draining swamps, then?" Toby asked, logically.

Allegra looked at her in surprise. "This is a mountain country," she said, and the girls immediately remembered they had spent hours on the train admiring those mountains. "There isn't a swamp within five hundred miles of here."

"We were just trying to be helpful. . . ." Andy said in embarrassed protest.

"Oh, but you *are* — you really *are*!" Allegra said earnestly.

"How?" Toby asked.

"You just gave me the best laugh I've had in weeks! Now, I've got to get to a fitting for my wedding dress. Here's a schedule of the official functions," she said, handing them each a list of parties and events, rendered in beautiful calligraphy. "First up is Great Aunt Agnes's tea. She's a Grand Duchess and a terrific lady. You'll be meeting my whole family, and James's as well, there. Also, you've each been assigned an escort for all the rest of the parties. The guys'll be there. I hope you'll get along." She winked at her friends, stood up, and walked gracefully out of the room.

"Guys?" Jane echoed in surprise. "I didn't realize we'd have dates — maybe they'll be royalty, too!"

"Probably just stuffy guys like Frederick," Andy said. Jane and Toby nodded in agreement. That *did* seem most likely.

CHAPTER
SIX

Andy smoothed an imaginary wrinkle out of the skirt of her yellow wool suit. She took a deep breath and followed Jane and Toby into the salon where Grand Duchess Agnes of Montavia was serving tea for the wedding party and special guests. Andy had looked at herself repeatedly in the three-section floor-length mirror before the Canby classmates had left their suite, but she couldn't believe that she was really prepared for a *Duchess's* tea party.

"You look fine," Jane whispered reassuringly.

"That's easy for you to say," Andy whispered back. "You were *born* going to fancy-schmancy tea parties. Remember the *Boston* Tea Party?"

"That was *before* I was born," Jane told her.

"What's the big deal about a tea party?"

Toby asked in her matter-of-fact way. "Just remember *not* to slurp, right?"

"Right," Jane said.

At that moment, Andy envied both of her friends — Jane for her social knowledge and Toby for not caring about it.

Fenster presented the girls to the assembled royalty.

"The demoiselles Andrea Cord, Jane Barrett, and October Houston," he said. The girls glanced anxiously at one another, unsure exactly how to act with such an introduction. Then it came to Andy. Gracefully, as the dancer she was, she stepped forward with her left foot and bent both knees in a deep curtsey, just as she would do one day at the end of a solo ballet performance. Jane and Toby quickly followed suit, but not so well.

"Bravo!" Allegra said, coming over to welcome them. "Now come meet Aunt Agnes." She took Andy's arm and led her over to their hostess.

A great aunt sounded to Andy like somebody who should have hankies stuffed in her sleeves, and a pair of glasses which pinched her nose. Aunt Agnes wasn't like that at all. In fact, Aunt Agnes was an extremely stylish woman in her late fifties who knew exactly how to put a guest at ease.

"That was an elegant entrance, my dear," she said warmly, shaking Andy's hand.

"Andy's a dancer, Aunt Agnes," Allegra explained. "I hope you'll see her dance soon. She's just wonderful, too. Someday, she'll be a prima ballerina. I know it." She turned to Andy. "You will dance at the reception, won't you?" she asked.

Andy could feel herself blushing with embarrassment at the praise, but before she could respond in any way, Allegra was turning in another direction.

"Oh, there's James," she said. "Excuse us please, Aunt Agnes. I must introduce him to my American friends."

For the next few minutes, Allegra had the girls' heads spinning with introductions. First there was James. As soon as they met, Andy could see why Allegra felt she was lucky. James *was* wonderful. He was everything Allegra said and more.

"Are you girls going to keep Allegra out of trouble here, too?" he asked, grinning. Obviously Allegra had told him about her adventures at Canby Hall in America.

"I'm not sure it's *out* of trouble that we kept her," Jane told him.

After that, the girls met both Allegra's and James's parents. Andy couldn't have imagined such an array of dukes and duchesses and earls all in one place.

"Boy, do I feel out of place," Andy told Jane while they stirred their tea daintily. "I think we're the only people here without titles!"

"Everybody in this country must be related," Toby said, looking at the crowd. "That's why they are all royalty."

"Yes," Jane mused. "Hundreds of royals and not one swamp to drain! What a waste!"

"Speaking of royals, Allegra is headed in our direction with a very royal-looking young man on her arm," Andy remarked. "And from the way she's looking at you, I think he's your escort."

Allegra was approaching them with her arm linked through that of a young man dressed in a regal suit, with a tri-color ribbon across his chest. He was tall and slender, dark-haired, with fine features.

"Not bad," Toby said, as if she were sizing up a horse.

"It's what's inside that counts," Andy reminded her, casually taking another bite of a cucumber sandwich.

"Jane Barrett, I would like to present His Royal Highness, Prince Armand of Almare — James's younger brother."

"How do you do?" Jane said, extending her hand to him.

He looked down his nose at her proffered hand as if he'd never seen one before. Jane pulled it back awkwardly.

"You don't shake hands with royalty," he said. "But I suppose you Americans aren't familiar with such protocol."

Jane was so astonished by this thinly veiled insult that she was, for a moment, speechless. But she'd spent her life around people who thought that their birthright was to be better than others and she knew that didn't necessarily make them better behaved. She also knew it was now her responsibility to establish cordial relations *and* to put him at his ease.

She smiled broadly at Prince Armand. "Oh, you're so right!" she told him. "There are so many things we don't know at all! Will you help me?"

For a moment, he looked at her, stunned. He glanced at Allegra, who was somehow containing a smirk, and then back at Jane. "Certainly," he said. With that, he took her hand, and tucked it around his arm, leading her off into the crowd.

"I knew she could do it!" Allegra said triumphantly. "She's perfect."

"What are you talking about?" Andy asked.

"Oh, it's just that Armand is a total, unforgivably snooty snob. He's such a snob that he doesn't think *I'm* good enough for his brother. Can you believe that? Well, I had to have somebody who could tame him through the wedding. Otherwise, he'll find some way to absolutely ruin it for us — and everybody else. Jane was the perfect candidate. She'll teach him a thing or two about breeding *and* diplomacy."

Allegra, Andy, and Toby looked to where Jane and Armand stood, near the buffet table. Armand was holding a saucer in one hand and a teacup in the other. He *appeared* to be showing Jane how to crook her pinkie finger while she drank tea.

"Wait'll she tells him about the tea party her family threw in Boston Harbor one day — as it were," Allegra grinned wickedly.

Just then, some long-lost relative claimed Allegra's attention. Before she left Andy and Toby, Allegra introduced them to another young man, a cousin of hers, named André. He was tall, like Armand, but that was where the resemblance stopped. He had a tan face and looked as though he spent most of his time out of doors. His blond hair was curly and rather unkempt. He seemed a bit uncomfortable with the formalities of the tea party, and as relieved as Andy and Toby to be talking to somebody who didn't have a title.

"Allegra tells me you come from Texas," he said to Toby.

"Rattlesnake Creek," she supplied. "My dad's ranch is just outside of town, but town isn't much more than a general store, a gas station, a few houses, and a church."

"You live on a ranch? A horse ranch?" he asked, his eyes lighting up.

"Yep. Horses and cattle." Toby was a girl of few words.

"I raise horses and train them," André told her. "Holsteiners — have you ever heard of them?"

"Oh, sure!" Toby said. "I ride western, of course, and most of our horses are quarter horses, but the Holsteiner breed is famous. Everybody is noticing them these days. In fact, I have a friend near school — his name is Randy — and he was telling me about this mare. . . ."

Andy couldn't believe it. Toby Houston could go for days on only a few words, but when it came to horses, she couldn't stop talking. All Andy knew about horses was that they were big animals, and they frightened her. She just didn't see the appeal, but it was obviously there, because at the first mention of the word "horse," André and Toby were best friends. That made Andy a crowd.

Excusing herself, though she didn't think André and Toby noticed, Andy wandered through the room, looking for a diversion. When she passed Armand and Jane, she heard Armand explaining to her why the Montavian impressionists were superior to the French, though less widely known. Andy wondered if Armand knew about the world-famous Barrett collection of impressionist paintings. Probably not. She steered clear of the pair, dreading being drawn into the conversation, especially when she heard Armand pronounce that throughout history art had only flourished because of royal patronage. Somehow, Jane managed a smile.

Andy grumbled and moved on. She meandered over to the tall French windows which opened onto a spacious marble terrace. It was too chilly to be outside, but it wasn't too chilly to look. The Montavian countryside was beautiful, even spectacular. From where she stood, she could see a valley, dotted with small but obviously prosperous farms. Beyond the valley, as a dramatic backdrop to the scene, majestic mountains pierced the sky.

The green of the valley, dotted with snow patches, led to rocky pastures, then to an evergreen forest topped by bare peaks. At the upper reaches of the mountains, the trees and terrain were completely covered with snow. On one of the mountains, there were telltale poles and wires, indicating the chairlift of a ski resort. Andy had only skied a couple of times in her life, each time at an artificially created hill near her Chicago home. It would be very different, indeed, to ski on a real mountain.

"Beautiful, isn't it?" a man's voice asked her. Startled, Andy turned around. What she saw almost took her breath away.

There stood a young man in a navy blue military uniform, which contrasted with the rich ebony hue of his skin. The uniform was decorated with gold buttons and braids and a couple of rows of medals and ribbons. But it was the young man's face that held her attention. It had a pronounced oval shape and a firm square jaw. His eyes were wideset and his brows were wonderfully uneven, one peaking ever so slightly. Even better than all that, the young man had the most merry gleam in his eyes, and the warmest smile Andy had ever seen.

Andy finally remembered her manners and answered his question. "Yes, it is beautiful," she said eagerly. Then she introduced herself. "I'm Andrea Cord," she told him.

"I know," he said. "I saw you enter — and from the moment you curtseyed I knew I had to meet you."

Andy's stomach felt very funny, and her knees nearly buckled. She'd never known a feeling like this before.

The man introduced himself. Andy could barely believe it. It turned out that his name was Ramad. He was the crown prince of a small principality on the Barbary Coast of North Africa.

"You mean where the eighteenth-century pirates came from?" Andy asked.

"The very place," he told her. "I don't think my own forebears were *actually* pirates, but I believe we made our family fortunes by offering those rascals hiding places in the caves on our rocky coastal palisades."

"You're not kidding, are you?" Andy asked.

"Not at all," he assured her.

"Well, me, I'm not a princess of anything — "

"Not yet," he interrupted her.

She looked at him quizzically and then went on to introduce herself. "I come from

Chicago, Illinois, U.S.A., and my parents own a restaurant. I work there sometimes."

"A restaurant!" he said. "And you *work* there! How wonderful! And one day you will own the family business?" he asked.

"Oh, no," she told him. "I will be a dancer, a ballet dancer."

"I *love* the ballet," he said. "Tell me about your dance studies."

Jane and Toby sometimes teased Andy that if the subject turned to dance, particularly ballet, she was like a record player that wouldn't stop. Always talkative, there was nothing Andy liked to talk about more than ballet, and it turned out, Ramad was very knowledgeable about it himself. Suddenly, it was as if the whole room were empty, except for the two of them.

For almost a half an hour, they talked about ballet. Andy told Ramad what she was learning and how they practiced, and he told her about ballet performances he had seen all over the world. She was completely entranced by the conversation and didn't even notice when Allegra began tugging at her sleeve.

"I think the princess wants to talk to you," Ramad told her, smiling that big warm smile that Andy had already decided was the most wonderful smile in the world.

"Oh," Andy said. For a moment, she couldn't even clear her mind enough to think who Allegra was. Then, with a sinking heart, she realized that Allegra had no doubt arrived to introduce her to *her* escort. Resigned, she pasted a smile on her face and turned to Allegra.

"Hi!" she said.

"Hi, yourself," Allegra retorted. "I've been looking for you two for twenty minutes because I wanted to introduce you, but I see you found each other without me."

"Found each other?" Andy said.

"I just knew you two would get along," Allegra said. "That's why you're sitting together at the dinners. That's all right, isn't it?" she asked.

"Oh, yes!" Andy said, more than pleasantly surprised. It was, after all, like a dream come true.

Assured that Andy and Ramad were acquainted, Allegra moved on to talk with more of Aunt Agnes's guests.

"Now, the Bolshoi," Ramad continued, as if they had not been interrupted. "That ballet troupe has a whole different feeling about it."

"You've seen the Bolshoi perform?" Andy asked.

"Only in London," he told her. "I was a guest of the palace and . . ."

As he continued describing the exquisite performance he'd seen, Andy realized she'd gotten it wrong. This wasn't a dream come true at all.

This was a *fairy tale* come true.

CHAPTER SEVEN

The next morning, the girls sat in their suite chatting. Jane was curled up on the brocade-covered sofa. Toby sat crosswise on a matching overstuffed chair, legs slung across the armrest. Andy, unusually quiet, sat on the chaise lounge, circling her bent knees with her arms, a dreamy look on her face.

Jane scrunched her nose in distaste. She looked to her friends for sympathy. "And *then* Prince Armand tried to tell me how difficult his life has been — like he's been burdened by having to live with so many *inferior* people around! Can you believe that? I've met a lot of snobs in my life, but he takes the cake!"

"So what did you say to him when he said that?" Toby asked.

Jane shrugged. "I just told him I knew *exactly* how he felt. He lapped it up!"

Toby giggled. "Allegra was right about you. He's awful, but you know how to handle him. She's a genius. She was also a genius pairing me up with André. Training show horses — Holsteiners is the breed he trains — is just fascinating!"

While Jane and Toby compared notes on their "escorts," Jane noticed that Andy was strangely silent. She'd seen Andy talking with Ramad all night. Now she seemed all talked out.

"Everything okay, Andy?" Jane asked.

Before Andy could answer there was a knock at the door.

"It's probably our royal breakfast," Jane said, standing up to open it. But when the door opened, instead of a tray of food, she was met by a garden of flowers — red, yellow, white, and pink roses — preceding Fenster into the room.

"Flowers for Miss Cord," Fenster announced.

"That's not just flowers," Toby remarked. "That's a whole greenhouse!"

"One dozen each," Fenster told them. "Where shall I put the vases?"

Suddenly alert, Andy bounced up and helped Fenster decide how to spread the wealth of beauty around the room. Then, when he had left, she took the envelope which had come with the flowers and pulled out the card.

"Oooh," she said breathlessly.

"Who are they from?" Toby demanded.

"Ramad," Andy said, reading the card. "He says he couldn't decide which color I would like best."

"How romantic! You must have knocked him off his feet!" Jane said, but then, looking more carefully at her friend, she realized she had it wrong, or at least she only had half the story. It was equally clear that Ramad had knocked Andy off *her* feet.

"Hey, Cord!" Toby said. "It's time for reality. Allegra said she and James would meet us in the ballroom at ten-thirty today. Our first job is to teach them to waltz well together — but I think when Allegra said *us*, she really meant *you*. I'll teach her square dancing."

"Oh, Armand will love *that*!" Jane remarked. "You should have heard him going on about peasant customs."

"Spare me," Toby said.

"I will," Jane assured her. "Now let's get this lovesick dancer to the ballroom."

Somehow, Jane and Toby managed to get Andy dressed. She followed them dreamily to the ballroom and arrived just as Allegra and James got there.

When it came to dancing, Andy was all business. Although what she knew best was ballet, there really wasn't any kind of dancing Andy couldn't do, including rock and roll, ballroom, and square dancing.

"All right, now, you both know how to waltz already, so we'll concentrate on making it look like you've been dancing together for years. James, put your right hand at the center of Allegra's back — like this — " she demonstrated, and then had Allegra rest her left hand lightly on his shoulder. "You've got to hear the one-two-three of the music." She nodded to Toby, who pushed Play on the cassette recorder, and they were off.

Jane watched. At first, it was hard to imagine that in only four days this halting performance of a waltz of sorts would be done for all of the invited guests to *the* royal event of the latter part of the century. Andy was waving her hands frantically and yelling out, "*One*-two-three, *turn*-two-three, *swirl*-two-three. No, no, you have to feel it. James, you go forward, Allegra, you have to trust him. Now, again. *One*-two-three!"

But after about a half an hour, it became apparent to Jane that Andy really did know what she was doing, for James and Allegra were doing a smoother waltz.

"You're going to have to practice more," Andy told them, "But I think you've probably learned about as much as you can absorb for today. I do want to show you some sweeping movements that can make the waltz rather elegant."

"Forget the sweeping motions," Allegra said. "The bottom line is that we have to waltz together for about three minutes, alone on the dance floor, and everybody should think that we dance so naturally together that it proves we were meant to be together."

"You will," Andy assured them. "Because it's true! One more time, then," she said and Toby pushed Rewind and Play once again.

As the couple swirled across the dance floor, the roommates watched interestedly. They were very pleased with what had been accomplished. It wasn't exactly "queening" lessons, but it was clear that they were being helpful to Allegra and that, after all, was what they wanted most.

Just as the music was drawing to an end, however, there was an interruption.

"What's this?" an indignant voice demanded from the doorway. Everybody looked over to see a red-faced Armand. "What *are* you doing?" he spoke to his brother.

"Allegra and I are waltzing, as you can plainly see," James told him, none too civilly. "Andrea has taught us so that we can dance at the upcoming balls. Didn't you like our waltz?"

"*I* wouldn't call it a waltz," Armand declared. "It may be called one in Chicago, Illinois," he pronounced the city's name with obvious distaste. "But in Almare, we have a more proper waltz. The great Almarian dancer, Boroloff, refined the dance several centuries ago." The girls exchanged glances, barely able to contain their laughter. Fortunately, Armand didn't notice. "Surely, brother, you remember it from our *own* dance instructor."

From the look on his face, it was clear that James sensed disaster. He didn't like the idea of his fiancée's friends being insulted — nor did he think that any one waltz was more refined than any other, but he couldn't risk a rift in the royal family.

"Ah, yes!" James told Armand, walking over to where he stood near the door. "But you remember these things so much better than I, Armand. It's now time for me to have a final fitting on my uniform. The epaulettes just haven't been sitting right. Come with me now, and refresh my memory of the justly famous Borolovian Waltz."

Armand's face beamed with victory. James put his arm across his brother's shoulder and led him out of the ballroom.

"Whew!" Allegra said, fanning herself with her hand. "That was a close one. Armand is almost impossible."

"Drop the 'almost,' Your Royal Highness," Jane said deferentially. "He's just plain impossible."

"Well, he's out of our hair for a while. Listen, let's forget about my creepy incipient brother-in-law. Let's have our lunch now and get down to business. Now that we've abandoned swamp draining, I can't wait to hear what else you have in mind for me!"

A few minutes later, they were all seated at a dining table in the royal apartments of the palace. The family quarters were a very pleasant surprise. In contrast to the enormous scale of the downstairs halls and even the girls' suites, the area Allegra and her parents lived in was comfortable and rather homey. The ubiquitous Fenster served the young women lunch, and they dug into the chicken salad hungrily, especially Allegra.

"Dancing is hungry work," Allegra remarked.

"And I guess pressing the Play button must be, too," Toby drawled, "because I'm eating every bit as much as you are. Or maybe it's just that the food is better than what we're used to at school. And speaking of school, queen school should be in session now."

"Oh, yes," Allegra said. "I saw you thumbing through that book while James and I were dancing, Jane. What have you come up with now?" she asked.

"First of all, we have to figure out how you'll handle the peasants," Jane began.

"Peasants?"

"Yeah, like the poor people," Andy explained.

"But there aren't any poor people here," Allegra told her. "We have such a successful tourist business — mostly skiing — that we even have to import labor. Our total population is less than twenty-five thousand people."

"There are neighborhoods in Chicago with more people in them," Andy remarked.

"Yeah, and several of the ranchers in our country have got more head of cattle than that," Toby contributed.

"Okay, so forget about the peasants, how about your justice system?"

"No problems."

"Foreign policy?"

"We're completely neutral. So's Almare," Allegra said.

Jane finished the last bite of her chicken salad. Laying her fork carefully on her plate, she regarded Allegra thoughtfully. "It seems to me that you don't really have any problems at all," Jane said. "Queening's going to be a breeze for you."

"You could be right, except for one thing," the princess said. "Don't forget Armand. He's a problem, isn't he?"

"Now, there I might have a suggestion for you," Jane said. "All last night, I kept thinking how much happier I would be if Armand were someplace else — like Siberia. How about a nice ambassadorship for him?"

"Oh, my!" Allegra exclaimed. "I think you've got it! That's it. Exactly the thing for him. Only instead of someplace cold and awful like Siberia, I think we should send him

him someplace warm and wonderful — like Nassau — that he would *never* want to leave. See, I *knew* you would be helpful to me."

"You mean figuring out how to get rid of a pain in your neck is part of queening?" Toby asked wryly.

"That's not exactly the way the royal protocol director would describe it, but it'll do," Allegra said. She began to rise from the table and Fenster sprang to her aid, helping her with her chair as if she couldn't do it herself. "Now, I have another fitting to go to this afternoon. I'll see you this evening at the dinner James's parents are giving. If you would like, Fenster can give you a tour of Almare this afternoon."

"In the royal wagon?" Toby asked, joking.

"Well," Allegra said. "It's awfully hard to see much from the roads. He'll take you in the royal helicopter if you would prefer. Right Fenster?"

"Certainly, Your Royal Highness," he said, bowing low as she walked out of the room.

CHAPTER EIGHT

That evening, Fenster drove Jane, Toby, and Andy to the palace in Almare. They were wearing evening gowns suitable for a royal do — at least as suitable as the wardrobes of all their school friends could make them.

Jane was in a cherry pink-silk dress, showing off her creamy skin and blonde hair. She wore gold slippers and carried a matching gold clutch purse. Andy had on a yellow chiffon gown that flowed behind her when she walked so that, Toby told her, it looked as if she were dancing with every step. She felt a tingle of excitement, knowing how good she looked, and sure that Ramad would know it, too.

Toby's dress was a deep rusty orange, almost a perfect match for her hair. With eyelet lace around the yoke, and the off-the-shoulder sleeves, the dress managed to create a distinctly Western American look — perfect for Toby.

"I feel like a princess," Andy confessed.

"And you look like one, too," Jane told her, confirming Andy's feelings about the dress.

"Do you think Ramad will like this color?" Andy asked, suddenly uncertain.

"From the way he was looking at you last night, to say nothing of the dozens of flowers you received this morning, I suspect that Ramad would think you were beautiful if you were wearing your Canby Hall field hockey uniform!" Jane said. "Now stop worrying and just enjoy the evening. After all, you have something fun to look forward to."

"So do *you*," Andy said cheerfully. "I mean, it isn't every day that you have the opportunity to spend time with somebody who is your social and intellectual superior the way Armand is!"

"Right. His blood isn't just blue — it's *ice* blue," Jane said.

"Golly, I thought you were a blue blood, too," Toby said.

"It's not just that, as you well know," Jane told her, "his Royal Snobbishness is a total pain in the neck. Did I tell you what he said about *Boston*? And, another thing. He felt it necessary to tell me — "

"Hold your fire," Andy warned. "We're coming up to the palace. Don't forget that Allegra's counting on you."

"Don't worry," Jane assured her friends. "I can't forget that because every time Armand opens his mouth, it's clear that all diplomatic relations between Almare and every other country in the world are at stake."

The car drew up to the gate of the Almarian palace. A man in a guard's dress uniform opened the car door and the girls began stepping out. Toby went first, then Andy. Behind her, she could hear Jane mumbling, " 'It is a far, far better thing that I do, than I have ever done.' "

"What's that?" Andy stage-whispered over her shoulder.

"It's from *A Tale of Two Cities* by Charles Dickens," Jane told her. "See, this guy is sacrificing himself for somebody else's happiness."

"I get the picture," Andy said. "So smile."

Jane pasted a gracious smile on her face and emerged, glowing, from the limousine.

"Your Majesties," Jane said, bobbing an abbreviated curtsey in greeting to the King and Queen of Almare. The girls were walking down the receiving line for the formal dinner. As host and hostess, James's parents were greeting the guests first.

"Ah, the American from Boston who has so captivated our young son!" the queen said.

Jane smiled politely. She even managed a blush as she wondered what Armand had *really* said about her. Gulping and collecting her thoughts, she recalled how the diplomatic future of the countries rested on her shoulders. "Prince Armand has been so helpful to me," she murmured. "Your Majesties cannot imagine how overwhelmed we poor colonials are by matters of court."

"Ah," the king remarked with a new understanding in his voice. "Has Armand been insulting you?"

"Oh, Your Majesty!" Jane uttered softly, knowing that was no answer at all.

The king winked at her and leaned toward Jane so that his wife could not hear him speak. "Listen," he said quietly. "Allegra tells me that you can handle the situation. Now that I've seen you in action, I know she knows what she's talking about. We're counting on you to keep him out of trouble."

Then, Jane blushed for real. "Yes, Your Majesty!" she said, and curtseyed to him. Without missing a beat, the king turned his eyes to his next guest with a welcoming smile and a firm handshake.

Jane suddenly got the feeling that although she might be a little short on information about "queening," she'd just learned a big lesson about "kinging." James and Armand's father was charming and smart — and it looked to her as if all the brains and charm had gone straight to James. Lucky for Allegra.

Before she even had a chance to breathe

deeply, Armand was at her side. "Won't you try some caviar?" he invited her, signaling a passing waiter. "The Almarian caviar is known throughout the world."

Jane sighed to herself. She had simply no interest in talking to Armand about fish eggs. But he was off on a long explanation about the Almarian cultivation of sturgeon.

Jane saw Allegra's parents approaching and tried to stop Armand from talking. Her efforts were in vain.

She curtseyed politely and greeted the king and queen by saying, "Good evening Your Majesties."

"You are interrupting me," Armand said pointedly, apparently unaware that the Montavians were by his side. Allegra's mother's eyebrow arched.

Jane didn't like the idea of insulting any of the royals standing around her, but she couldn't let Armand insult the Montavians. "I beg your forgiveness, Your Highness," she began.

"Granted," he snapped, thinking she was apologizing, and then he went right on. "The Almarian-trained sturgeon breeders — "

The queen cleared her throat.

" — I certainly hope nobody here is coming down with the flu, or worse," Armand grumbled in response to the throat clearing, before he continued his monologue on caviar. The queen's eyebrow shot higher.

Jane gave up on protocol. It wasn't working. "Armand," she said sharply. "The king and queen of Montavia are at your side."

Finally, Armand stopped talking. He glanced to where Allegra's parents stood and then, rather than offering them the greeting their station deserved, the prince simply clicked his heels together and nodded his head in their direction.

Apparently, Armand's chronic rudeness was nothing new to Allegra's family. Jane saw that Allegra's mother was trying to hide a smile. That still didn't make it all right and Jane felt badly that she hadn't been able to insulate Allegra's family from Armand's insult. After all, that was what she was there for. She was trying to figure out how she could possibly have kept Armand from doing what he had done when suddenly she realized that there was much greater danger ahead.

"Say, my boy!" Allegra's father was uttering jovially, slinging an arm across Armand's shoulder. "We're doing a little skeet shooting tomorrow. Won't you join us?"

Jane knew what skeet shooting was. A group of people, armed with rifles, shooting at chunks of clay which have been catapulted into the sky. It was sort of a simulation of bird hunting, but when it came to Armand, the critical issue was that it meant Armand would be near a lot of important people, and armed with live ammunition.

"Why, I'd love that, Your Majesty!" Armand said enthusiastically. "In fact, I've just gotten a new rifle I'd like to try out. There's this Almarian gunsmith . . ." he began.

Suddenly, Jane had an awful image of the terrible things which could go wrong. Surely, she would be needed.

"Your Majesty," she said, interrupting Armand and earning a dirty look from him for her trouble. "May I come, too?"

The king looked at her in surprise, and then a broad grin crossed his face. "Of course you may, my dear," he said warmly.

Jane smiled outwardly. Inwardly, she sighed. And then her mind began racing. What *would* she wear?

"I really feel sorry for Jane, don't you?" Toby asked.

"Hmmm?" Andy responded idly. Her eyes were scanning the crowd in the large room. There were hundreds of faces there, but not the one she was looking for.

"I said I feel sorry for Jane," Toby repeated. "Armand is quite a handful."

"Oh," Andy said.

"I guess we'll be having cement for supper again tonight, don't you think?" Toby asked, realizing that Andy hadn't heard a word she'd said.

"I suppose so," Andy replied dreamily.

Toby gave up and began scanning the room as well. She spotted Ramad nearing the end of the receiving line. "He's over there," she said. "And he's just spotted you. He'll be here within fifteen seconds."

"Who will?" Andy asked innocently.

Toby gave her a withering look and then stared at her watch. "Fourteen," she said, just before Ramad bowed to Andy, taking her hand and kissing it. For a moment, Toby was afraid that Andy was going to faint, but she realized that even if she did, Ramad would be only too happy to catch her, pick her up, and walk off dramatically with her, presumably, as the camera drew back, allowing the couple to disappear into the sunset.

It was all she could do to keep from grumbling because it was clear as a bell that as far as the two of them were concerned, there were really only two people in the whole ballroom. When Toby shrugged and walked off, she was sure that neither Andy nor Ramad noticed her departure.

"Oh, there you are, Toby!" a familiar voice called to her from around a pillar and a waiter. "I've been looking for you." She turned to see André, a most welcome sight. "I spotted one of your friends attempting to save diplomatic relations between Montavia and Almare."

"Poor Jane," Toby groaned sympathetically.

"I thought you said she was rich," André teased. Toby smiled at him. He was an awfully nice boy, able to joke about serious things without making them seem trivial. "And your other friend and Prince Ramad seem to be walking about six inches off the ground."

"Well, after all, she is a dancer," Toby told him. "Always has been light on her feet, you know?"

"Speaking of such things, I have looked at the royal schedule for tomorrow and it seems, amazingly, that nothing is scheduled for you at all. Would you like to go horseback riding with me?"

"You mean get away from all this fancy palace finery, lovely gowns, elegant food, perfect servants, and just go ride horses out of doors?" Toby asked.

André nodded.

"You bet I would!"

"This is such a pretty country, Ramad, do you know that?" Andy asked him a few minutes later. They were once again standing near the windows, this time looking out on another range of mountains, different, but equally beautiful to the ones they had admired together the night before.

"I know it is, but it always seems when I am here that I hardly have time to admire the beauty of the country. Now, with you, Andy . . ."

His words trailed off. Andy could feel a little tingle in her stomach.

"Have you ever skied here?" she asked him.

"Oh, yes. The skiing in both Almare and Montavia is wonderful. Would you like to try it?" he asked.

"Sure, but I don't know when I would have the chance," she replied.

"How about tomorrow? I'm sure you have the day to yourself. The prince and princess are working together on their own parts of the wedding. The rest of the wedding party is completely at liberty. Miss Cord," he said, addressing her formally, "would you accompany me on a skiing trip to Montavia tomorrow? I know the most wonderful mountain."

"Will it be dangerous?" she asked. She meant, was it dangerous for a future ballet dancer.

"No," he assured her, understanding what she was asking. "I'll take no chances with this beautiful ballet-star-to-be."

"Then it sounds perfect," said Andy. She looked at him. "Just perfect."

CHAPTER NINE

The next morning, the guest suite at the Montavian palace was strewn with clothes. None of the Canby girls, in packing, had anticipated the day's activities of skeet shooting, horseback riding, and skiing.

"What *does* the well-dressed woman wear skeet shooting?" Jane groaned. She was standing in front of the mirror. So far, her outfit consisted of a tweed skirt, cashmere turtleneck sweater, tall brown leather boots, and a soft brown leather jacket.

"Hey, Jane, relax. You know perfectly well that whatever you decide to wear, an *Almarian* designer has done it better," Toby teased her.

"You're right. I can't win, so I might as well relax. The real problem is that if I'm standing next to Armand and he gets too obnoxious, and there's a loaded gun — "

"So much for diplomatic relations, huh?" Toby said.

"Try this," Andy said, handing her a large paisley scarf.

Jane took the scarf, folded it into a triangle, and drew it around her shoulder. "Good colors!" she said, admiring how the rust and brown tied in the other colors of her outfit. "Now all I need is a pin. . . ."

"How about a horse head?" Toby offered, fishing one out of her drawer.

"Perfect!" Jane announced, satisfied. Then she backed away from the mirror and let Toby take the floor.

Since Toby always traveled with boots and jeans, whether she expected to ride or not, it was easier to outfit her than her friends. "André will be wearing breeches and high boots — English style," she said. "But riding's riding, and these clothes will do." She donned a Canby Hall sweatshirt, her Texas style riding hat, and declared herself ready.

Andy took a little longer. The girls had sweaters and even a windbreaker among them, but there weren't any skiing pants and there didn't seem to be an adequate substitute. Andy was nearly shaking with nervousness and anticipation and not at all happy at the prospect of being improperly dressed. Finally, Toby came up with the perfect solution: Fenster.

She rang for him, and he appeared almost

instantly. When the problem was put in his hands, he nodded, said, "Very well, miladies," bowed, and disappeared. Within seconds, he reappeared with a selection of ski pants from Allegra's wardrobe. Allegra and Andy were close enough in size that the fit was nearly perfect. Andy selected the pale blue ones because they went so well with Jane's heavy sweater and Toby's windbreaker.

"Hey, I'm going to need something for *après ski*," she said.

"*Après ski!*" Jane echoed. "There won't be any *après ski*, Andy. You're supposed to practice your dance solo this afternoon and then we've got a dinner dance to go to tonight."

"I didn't mean for tonight. I just meant for this afternoon," Andy explained.

"But what about your rehearsal?" Toby reminded her. "Fenster says the ballroom will be available between four and six this afternoon so you can practice your solo."

"Oh, no problem," Andy said airily. "We'll be back in plenty of time for that."

"Are you sure? You two seem so far in the clouds when you're together that it's a wonder you don't run off to his little principality to live happily ever after!" Jane said.

"Give me a break! I'll get everything done, and I'll be everywhere I'm supposed to be today," Andy promised. "First I'll go skiing, then I'll practice for a couple of hours, then we'll all dress for the dinner dance. You'll see. It'll work out just fine."

Jane was about to remind Andy that her watch was still set on Canby Hall time — six hours behind Montavia — when Fenster knocked. Prince Ramad was waiting for Miss Cord in the morning room.

"Ooooh," Andy cooed, following Fenster out of the room.

Jane and Toby exchanged knowing looks.

"I'm worried about her, you know?" Jane said.

"Me, too," Toby nodded. "She reminds me of a cowboy I once knew who fell in love with a princess. They were both perfectly nice people, but the only thing that happened when they fell in love was that they made each other miserable, and everybody around them as well."

"I was thinking the same thing," Jane said.

At that moment, Andy's thoughts were far from those of her friends. Ramad held her arm as they walked from the morning room and into the waiting car. Andy loved the excitement she felt at his nearness, and the warm glow of his eyes when he looked at her.

"I really haven't skied much," she said.

"To tell you the truth, Andy, there isn't much snow in my country, but I have learned some things. We won't do anything dangerous."

She returned his gaze, unable to do anything to wipe the silly grin off her face.

After a short drive, they arrived at the luxurious ski resort in Almare. They entered through a large lobby, lushly carpeted. The floor-to-ceiling windows looked out on the breathtakingly beautiful mountains, shown off to advantage in the day's sparkling sunshine.

Andy and Ramad were quickly fitted with boots and skis and, right after their skis were snapped into place, they were whisked onto an airborne chair taking them to the top of the beginners' hill.

"The last time I was on something like this was at a carnival," Andy told Ramad.

"You were skiing at a carnival?" he asked, confused.

"Oh, no," Andy giggled. "I wasn't on a ski lift — it was a ferris wheel. It was nighttime, and I was riding with one of my brothers. When we got up to the top, we could see for miles. The whole fairground was below us, but we could also see the lights from the nearby town, too. It was great. Until my brother started rocking the darn thing!"

"You mean like this?" Ramad teased, swaying the lift.

"*Exactly* like that," she said. "And I'll thank you to stop it right now."

"Anything for you," Ramad said, suddenly serious, stilling the rocking wooden seat and keeping it smooth for the rest of the ride. Perched high above the snowy hill, gazing at the world below, Andy felt just like a Snow Princess.

Then she got to the top of the hill. When the chair lift reached the peak, there was a ranger to help her off the lift, but suddenly the skis, which looked so graceful on other people, were an impossibly clumsy burden to her. She tried stepping forward, but the skis were a big weight on her foot, as if she'd stepped on a shoe lace. She stumbled. Ramad caught her.

"I'm never going to be able to do this!" Andy predicted.

"That's what everybody says," Ramad assured her. "Come on now. It's not as if you walk. What you do is slide — rather like on ice skates. For now, we'll stay on level land and then, when you think you're ready for it, we'll try a little hill."

Andy was so eager to be with Ramad that, even though she didn't think she'd ever be able to manage the skis, she did what he told her. She found that, by sort of walking on her toes and sliding, and by using the poles for balance, she could, in fact, move forward. She didn't look anything like any of the skiers she saw on the slopes, but at least she was standing up.

"Why, Andy, you're very good!" Ramad

complimented her. "I know you're not quite Olympic material yet, but you haven't broken any bones so far, either!"

"Oh, what a thought," Andy said, trudging along behind him. "That's a dancer's nightmare, you know?" she said.

"You're serious about your dancing, aren't you?" he asked.

"Yes, dancing is the most important thing in the world to me. I love to watch it, as you know, but even more, I love to do it. It makes me feel as if I am completely free and completely in control of myself. Sometimes, I think I could leap as high as the Empire State Building. It doesn't matter that I can't. It does matter that I sometimes feel that way."

"You have such wonderful individuality," Ramad said. "You care about something important — "

"Important to *me*, that's for sure," Andy said.

"And to me, too," Ramad said.

Andy followed him across the flat area through a small grove of trees, to an open space with a very slight hill. Ramad paused at the top of the hill, then bent his knees and pushed off with his poles. Andy watched as he swept across the snow smoothly. It looked so easy.

She stood at the top of the slope, and looked down. Even if she fell, she could hardly hurt herself on such a gentle slope. She took a deep breath and pushed off.

Reason told her she wasn't going very fast, but she could feel the wind on her face and in her hair. She breathed in the cool freshness, and it was as exhilarating to her as leaping across the stage. Too soon the slope leveled off and she came to a slow stop next to Ramad.

"Oh!" she said, surprised to be still again. "That was wonderful!" She grinned with joy.

He grinned back at her. "Come on, now, I'll show you how to climb back up and we can try it again."

Andy quickly got the knack of side stepping up the hill and she and Ramad went up and down the little slope several more times. When they got tired, they sat down on a small bench in the grove of trees.

"I think I'll be willing to try a little steeper hill in a few minutes," she told him.

"I knew you'd take to this, Andy. I'm glad we can enjoy it together. I like sharing things with you."

"You give me chills when you say things like that, you know," Andy said. "You're so serious."

"It's true," he agreed. "Sometimes I *am* serious. My brothers think I am too solemn, but that's only fair, because I think they are silly children!"

"Tell me about your country," Andy encouraged him. "Tell me about your family — about being a prince."

"You want me to tell you what I want to

be when I grow up?" he teased.

"Yeah, I guess so," she said, smiling back at him.

"Mine is a small country, you know, but my family is responsible for its well-being. We have some fertile lands and good farming. We have mining, too, so our land is rich for us." He stopped talking and looked at Andy quizzically. "Am I saying something funny to you?"

"Not really," she said, suppressing a grin. "But you sound a little like a geography lesson. Tell me more about *you*, about your family, about your home."

"Sometimes I do that, I know," he said. "I get so used to representing my people that I sometimes forget to represent myself. I'll try harder, though." And he began again. He told Andy about his family's home — the one they had lived in for hundreds of years. He told her about the mountains he could see from his own bedroom window — how different they were from the ones in front of them now. He told her about the Rhodesian Ridgeback dogs he raised and named after painters. "Van Gogh is the sly one," he told her. "He will get my servant to feed him and then he comes to me all moon-eyed, trying to trick me into feeding him again. It worked for a while, until he began putting on a lot of weight — then we got wise to him."

"That's exactly the same thing my little

sister Nancy used to do — only in our family, she had a lot more than two of us to go to for a snack, especially in the restaurant!"

"I like the things you tell me about your family, Andy. I think I would like to meet them someday."

"Oh, you would like them!" Andy assured him. "They're wonderful."

"Yes, I think so," he said, taking her hand in his and looking deep into her eyes. "And you will come to my country, too," he said. It wasn't a question, it was a statement. His certainty nearly took her breath away, and she remembered Jane's remark about living happily ever after in Ramad's country. The very idea that Ramad might be thinking the same thing frightened her.

"Come on," she said, standing up on her skis again and changing the subject. "Let's try a steeper hill. I'm ready for the big time!"

"All right!" Ramad agreed enthusiastically.

He led her across the clearing and through another grove. She followed him carefully, but her heart was beating so fast she could hardly breathe.

What would Ramad's country be like? *His* castle? *His* family? *His* dogs? Was it beautiful? Could she ever learn to love another land and another family as she loved her own? Her thoughts were racing even more quickly than her heart. She barely noticed as they came out onto an open trail which led down to the bottom of the hill. Following Ramad automatically, she pushed forward with her poles, but her few practice runs on the gentle slope just weren't enough training for the hill in front of her, especially when her right ski jumped up over a bump in the snow. All of a sudden, she completely lost her balance. Andy's arms swing wildly, first correcting, then overcorrecting her imbalance. Finally, to avert disaster, she sat down on the backs of her skis, but that didn't stop her from skiing! She began to slide straight down the hill as if she were on an old-fashioned sled, with her backside as the third runner.

She tried calling out to Ramad, but he was concentrating on his own skiing so hard that he couldn't hear. Then, as she watched, Ramad slowed down and turned just enough to be exactly in front of her. Closer and closer she came, finally bumping smack into him and knocking the crown prince into a snowdrift!

Andy couldn't believe what she had done. "Oh, Ramad, I'm so sorry!" she cried. "Are you all right? Did I hurt you?"

Slowly, Ramad lifted his head from the snowy slope, wiping flakes off his face with his hand. For a moment, he stared at Andy in total surprise and then Andy began laughing. He laughed with her, his deep hearty amusement ringing out in the cold mountain air.

"No, my Andy," he said, "I'm not hurt at all. Here let me help you up." First he pushed himself up, being careful not to let his skis fly out from under him. Then he offered both hands to Andy. She took his hands and rose cautiously. When she was standing, she found that she was very, very close to Ramad.

She looked up at him. He looked down into her eyes. Then, his arms encircled her and he leaned down. When their lips met Andy was aware of the most wonderful warming feeling she had ever known in her life.

CHAPTER TEN

"Andy, where have you *been*?" Jane asked in an accusing tone. It was almost seven o'clock and the dinner dance was scheduled to begin in forty-five minutes. Andy, still garbed in her skiing clothes, had just walked in the door of the suite.

Both Toby and Jane were in the process of getting dressed for the party. Jane, wrapped in a terry cloth robe, was carefully applying her makeup at the mirror in the vanity. Toby was working vigorously on her hair, trying to eke some glamour out of its annoyingly singleminded curliness.

"I've been skiing with Ramad, as you know perfectly well," Andy retorted.

"But you missed your practice time this afternoon," Toby reminded her.

"Oh, I don't need to practice," Andy said. "I've spent hundreds of hours on that old solo. Two hours more or less, one way or another, isn't going to make any difference. Anyway, I don't even know if I'll be *doing* the solo. Ramad told me today that in his country, a woman would never show so much of herself in public as a ballerina does. Her beauty is saved only for her husband. Isn't that something?"

"Something is the word, all right," Toby said. "But exactly what kind of something is another question."

"The only something I know right now is that we've got to do something about you and your clothes so you can be ready for the dinner dance in less than an hour. It's out of the question to be late for a do like this. Royal command performance, and all, don't you know?" Jane reminded her friends.

Toby thought Jane sounded like she'd been spending too much time with Armand, but she had a point. They couldn't be late for the party. The two girls shooed Andy into the shower and then laid out her clothes for her to help speed up the dressing process.

Forty-three minutes later, the three girls appeared at the door of the Montavian Palace Ballroom. Every last bit of makeup had been applied. Every hair was in place. Nobody noticed that Andy was still breathing hard from rushing so much.

That night's party was very different from

the others. For one thing, there were two separate parties going on, one for the older generation, taking place in Almare, and this one for the younger generation, James's and Allegra's friends and contemporaries, in Montavia. Instead of the usual string orchestra, there was a disc jockey. The ballroom was decorated like a disco, complete with lasers and flashing lights on the floor. As each guest arrived, they were given glow-in-the-dark plastic strings which they could wear around their necks, ankles, wrists, or as crowns. The music was loud and boisterous, and the feeling was pure fun. For the first time since they'd left Massachusetts, the roommates felt in their own element.

"Boy, Cary would love this!" Jane said as she snapped a neon string around her neck. Cary Slade was a boyfriend of Jane's, and lead guitarist in a punk band called Ambulance.

"Sure Cary would," Toby agreed. "But the question of the day is what will *Armand* think of it?"

"Did somebody call my name?" Armand said, coming up to the girls. He was wearing a tuxedo, as were all of the men, but he was also wearing a necktie made of the glowing plastic, plus a neon monocle. The overall effect was positively silly. "Do you like the style?" he asked, posing as if he were in a fashion show.

The girls had a hard time containing their surprise. "Looks fantastic, Armand," Jane said.

"Never saw anything like this at home," he said. "It's great stuff. What fun. But enough talk. We're all seated at the same table. Follow me."

He led them through the ballroom to the head table, where Allegra, James, André, and Ramad were already seated.

"Neat, huh?" Allegra asked her American friends. They weren't sure whether she meant the sudden, and welcome, change in Armand, or the whole setup for the party. It didn't really matter to them, though, because it was *all* neat.

"Everything is just fabulous!" Jane said, slipping into the chair Armand held for her. "How did you do it?"

Allegra grinned slyly. "James and I had talked about having a party like this for our friends, but it was difficult getting our parents to go along with it. It took tact, diplomacy, statesmanship, subtlety, negotiation skill, savoir-faire, and maneuvering."

"And you're looking to *us* for lessons in queening?" Toby asked aghast. "You got it locked, Allegra. No sweat."

Armand gave her a funny look. It appeared to Jane that when the situation was completely un-Almarian, it was acceptable to Armand for it to be different, but that still wouldn't make it acceptable for a lady to use slang like "no sweat." Armand had a long way to go.

"So, now, here's my first queenly decree: Everybody tell me what fun things they did today. Toby, you first."

All attention turned to Toby. It was never easy for Toby to talk to a group, except when the subject was horses. She and André told their friends about riding. "Well," she began. "This place is *nothing* like Rattlesnake Creek." Then, because it was such a funny thing to have said, even she began laughing. Pretty soon, she and André were describing the countryside and the differences between Western riding in Texas and English riding in Montavia.

"I don't have to ask about the skeet shooting," Allegra said. "James was there, and he tells me that he was the best."

"Ahem!" Armand responded. "I take exception to that allegation."

"Oh, you do, do you, little brother?" James teased. "I suppose just because you managed to hit a few of those clay chunks, you fancy yourself to be the best in the land?"

"Jane to the rescue!" Allegra said from across the table. "Who *was* the best?"

"Why, that's easy, Allegra," Jane said smoothly. "Your father, our host, His Royal Majesty King Rudolph of Montavia."

Allegra grinned at her. "Of course," she said. "And don't tell me there isn't anything

I can't learn about diplomacy from you!"

Everybody laughed then.

At that moment, the music started. Although this was a relatively informal formal party, Allegra and James knew that nobody would dance until they danced first. They excused themselves from their guests of honor and walked out onto the dance floor.

André turned to Andy. "Toby tells me that she and Jane visited your family in Chicago over a vacation — and worked in the restaurant."

"Oh, yes," Andy said. "It was great to have them there. In fact, it's always great to be with my friends. We do some pretty wild things together sometimes!"

"Such as?" he encouraged her.

Andy wrinkled her forehead, trying to decide which of their adventures to share. "Well, there was the time we raised money with a Halloween party — "

"And don't forget our ghost hunt!" Toby added. "And our stint as interior decorators."

"Oh, no!" Andy groaned. "I could never forget that!"

The girls told André, Armand, and Ramad about some of their adventures together, both in school and out of it. They told about their visit to Toby's ranch and to Jane's family home. Once they started talking about Canby Hall, it was hard to stop them. Soon the girls were all laughing, and both Armand and André were laughing along with them.

"No wonder Allegra wanted to go to school with you three!" André remarked.

"And no wonder her parents wouldn't permit it!" Armand added.

Jane looked at him. She felt that, for tonight at least, she was seeing a very different young man from the one she'd been coping with for several days now. She also had no doubt that he'd start being his own usual stuffy, boring, and snobbish self in the morning — once he was back into the usual formal routine instead of in the night's almost fairyland disco.

Then Jane turned to Ramad, the young prince who seemed to have captured Andy's heart. His face was solemn, in sharp contrast to the smiles and giggles from all of the other occupants of the table. Jane wondered what was going on in his mind.

"Ramad," she began. "We've been yacking about our homes, but I'm afraid I know almost nothing about yours. Tell me about it."

He appeared startled to have been asked. Jane was afraid, for a moment, that she'd somehow breached protocol. Was she supposed to call him Your Highness? It didn't seem likely, considering the general informality of even the stiffest formalities on this special night.

"There really isn't much to tell," he said

quietly and Jane knew better than to ask any more. He obviously wasn't in a mood to talk. "I think we can dance now," Ramad said, rising from his chair. "Andy, would you care to?"

Andy stood up, and they walked to the dance floor together. Jane watched them and wondered. She'd never seen her friend Andy so dreamy about anybody, and it was clear that Ramad felt the same way about Andy. But there was another side to their romance, too. Normally levelheaded and responsible, Andy was becoming more than a little irresponsible. It wasn't like her to miss practice at any cost, especially when her royal command performance could be so important to her career. After all, their whole reason for being in Montavia was Allegra's wedding, not Andy's romance with Ramad.

Ramad was a fine dancer. The two of them moved in near perfect unison, as if they'd been born to dance with one another. Jane was so entranced with their dancing that she didn't hear Armand the first time he spoke to her.

"Ahem!" he said sharply, finally gaining her attention. "Would you be good enough to dance with me? The next piece to be played is an American rock song. Will you show me the proper way to dance to it?"

All thoughts of Andy and Ramad fled

from Jane's mind in her total astonishment at Armand's request. *Will wonders never cease?* Jane asked herself, standing up from the table and following the prince to the dance floor.

CHAPTER ELEVEN

"Good morning!" Allegra greeted the girls brightly, stepping into their suite. Toby, Andy, and Jane were eating the breakfast Fenster had delivered a few minutes earlier.

"Good morning to you," Jane returned. "Come join us. We were just talking about what a wonderful party that was last night."

"Yes, it was, wasn't it?" Allegra asked, smiling. "It was just exactly what I wanted. I'm glad if you all had fun."

"It was so good, even old *Armand* had fun!" Jane told her.

"Well, that particular magic spell has broken. He's already telephoned me once this morning."

"What for?" Toby drawled.

"To remind me that according to *Almarian* wedding customs I'm supposed to say 'I shall' instead of 'I do.' Can you imagine?"

Jane nodded her head. "Yep, that's our Armand. Back to normal. At least *I* don't have to spend any more time with him until tonight."

"Well, *I* do — or should I say 'I shall'?" Allegra joked. "We've got the final wedding rehearsal this afternoon and of course, he'll be there. And," she said, turning to Andy. "Speaking of that — I know you missed your dance practice time yesterday afternoon. I was hoping you would be able to do your solo tonight at some point in the rehearsal dinner. The ballroom *is* available for practice this morning. Would you like to use it?"

"Oh, no," Andy said quickly. "I can't practice this morning. Ramad is meeting me and we're going for a hike and then he's planned a lunch for us at a little place he knows about. What time is the wedding rehearsal?" The look on Andy's face told everyone that Andy knew she would be cutting it tight.

"The rehearsal begins at one-thirty," Allegra said. "We have a lot to go through, so it will take the full afternoon. You won't have any other time to practice your solo. Will you be able to perform tonight without a practice?"

Andy shook her head. "Allegra," she began. "I haven't danced at all since we left Canby Hall. I'm going to be so stiff. I just don't see how I can — "

Jane and Toby looked at her in surprise. It just wasn't like Andy to decline a chance to dance for *any* reason. Something was going on, and Andy's roommates and Allegra didn't like it.

"I'm sorry to disappoint you," Andy told Allegra.

"That's okay," Allegra said. "You know best about what you can do. I was just hoping it would work out." Allegra shrugged her shoulders. Jane could tell she was trying to make it look as if she didn't really care. Jane didn't believe her act.

"Look," Allegra said, standing up from the table. "I've got an appointment with the manicurist now. I'll be back here after that. You'll be here, won't you, Jane and Toby?" They nodded. "Okay, then we can spend the morning together, while Andy romps around the mountains with her handsome prince!"

"See you then," Toby told her.

When Jane was sure Allegra was out of earshot, she turned to Andy. "What *are* you doing?" she demanded. "Allegra invited you here to dance for her and to be in her wedding. She didn't invite you here to spend all your time with Ramad! Can't you see that you hurt her feelings — and after all she's done for us!"

Andy's face was stony. "Well I'm sorry if I hurt her feelings, but I *can't* dance cold, as you know — "

"But you wouldn't *have* to if you spent this morning practicing, instead of climbing mountains."

Andy pushed her chair back from the table and stood up. She grabbed her sweater and jacket from the sofa where she'd put them and walked toward the door. Before she reached it, she turned to Jane. "If you know so much about ballet, why don't *you* do the solo instead?" she asked sarcastically. With that, she turned and walked out the door of the suite.

"Whew!" Toby sniffed. "What's got into that little dogie?"

"A royal pain in *our* necks, I think," Jane said.

"My guess is we're in for more trouble," said Toby.

"Not if we keep our mouths shut," Jane told her.

"Sounds like the best idea," Toby agreed.

By the time Allegra returned, Toby and Jane had finished their breakfasts and gotten dressed. Jane, normally a very untidy person, had finally been embarrassed into tidiness by the three chambermaids who had come to clean the suite up the day before.

Since it was a casual morning and neither of them had plans for the afternoon, they had just put on jeans and sweaters. Toby wore her usual boots. Jane had on argyle socks and Reeboks.

Allegra reentered the suite waving her hands to dry her nails. "I tried to get Tanya to paste sparkly things on each nail, but she wouldn't do it," Allegra said, joking.

"Is that a Montavian tradition?" Jane asked.

"No, and it's not an Almarian one, either. Listen," she continued, "speaking of Almarian traditions, I've had a couple more phone calls from Armand this morning. He interrupted my manicure several times. He's been asking questions about toasts and things like that at the wedding breakfast. What's a best man?" Allegra asked Jane.

"Oh, that's what Americans call the head groomsman at a wedding. That's what Armand is at yours, right?"

"James's father insisted. Usually, it should be the groom's best friend, and believe me, Armand is *not* James's best friend."

"Well, you've got me to blame for the questions. Armand stopped talking about Almare long enough last night to ask about America. He was very interested in a lot of American wedding traditions. So I was telling him things like how the best man makes a toast to the bride and groom. And other things, like tin cans, and the bride's garter, and shivarees — you know — things like that."

"Like *what*?" Allegra asked.

Suddenly, Jane paled. She realized that in response to Armand's unexpected friendliness, she'd played completely into his hand! She'd given him at least three ways to make Allegra and James completely miserable at their own wedding!

"Oh, no," Jane groaned.

"Is this bad news?" Allegra asked.

"Could be," Jane confessed. "But if I've messed it up, I promise I'll make it up to you."

"What are you talking about?"

"Well, I got sort of carried away," Jane said. "I got to telling Armand how much fun American weddings are — like how the best man sometimes does like to play practical jokes?"

"Practical jokes?" Allegra echoed, realizing the potential of an idea like that in Armand's hands.

Jane nodded sheepishly. "Like he sometimes ties a bunch of tin cans on the back of the car the bride and groom are leaving in. But before that, he has to make a toast at the reception — and it's often funny, sometimes a little insulting, jokingly, I mean."

"I don't like the sound of this," Allegra said.

"Neither do I," Jane told her. "At least in the light of day. Last night, it seemed pretty innocent."

"Innocent in anybody's hands, except those of Armand," Allegra said.

"I'm getting the idea of that now."

"Okay, so that's two. What's the third thing? Shivaree?"

"On the wedding night, a whole bunch of people are supposed to get noisemakers, like pots and pans, and stand outside where the couple is staying and make a lot of noise."

"They do this in Boston?" Allegra asked in surprise.

"Oh, *never* in Boston," Jane assured her. "I've just read about shivarees."

"And do they do this in Texas?" Allegra asked Toby.

"No *ma'am*," Toby replied. "I've never even read about this thing. What we do in Texas is to have a square dance with Parrish McCoy doing the calling. That's lots of fun. No trouble at all."

"Parrish McCoy? Squares? What *are* you talking about?"

"I could explain," Toby said, "but for now, I just wish that I'd been the one talking to Armand last night, not Jane."

Allegra sighed and leaned back in the brocade upholstered chair. "To be perfectly honest, both James and I have suspected all along that Armand was going to do something which would be a total nuisance at the wedding. The only question, really, has been exactly *what* he was going to do. Now, it's perfectly possible that we have an advantage, because I think we know *what* he's going to do."

"And forewarned is forearmed!" Jane announced.

"That's the idea," Allegra said. "Now all

we have to do is be one step ahead of him."

"Look, Allegra," Jane said. "Armand is my problem. You leave him to me. You and James are in charge of having fun. Toby and Andy will help me with keeping Armand from messing it up for you, okay?"

"I'm sure I couldn't be in better hands," Allegra said.

Jane wished she had all of Allegra's confidence in them, but she didn't want Allegra to worry about something she couldn't do anything about in the first place.

"Okay, then tell me about Parrish McCoy doing the calling," Allegra said.

For the next half hour, Toby and Jane took turns describing weddings, American style — from Texas square dances to the throwing of the bridal bouquet.

"Don't forget about 'Something old, something new, something borrowed, something blue'!" Toby said, and then Jane explained the tradition.

"Right, and 'Change the name and not the letter; change for worse and not for better.' That means if your last names have the same initial, you shouldn't get married. But that's a silly one, too," Toby said.

"Oh, they are *all* silly, of course, but they are wonderful things!" Allegra said. "Your weddings have such fun in them — not so much pomp like ours — or at least like the one James and I are going to have. I mean, I know it's necessary to follow all the stuffy traditions for a royal wedding like this, but if only — well, maybe," she said, and her voice drifted off.

"Now you're beginning to sound like Armand," Jane accused her.

Allegra's eyes opened wide. "Anything but that!" she screeched, and tossed a silk-covered pillow at Jane. Jane ducked and the pillow sailed past her, just missing a crystal lamp by inches.

"Don't worry," Allegra assured her. "It's Almarian crystal — a gift from James's great grandfather to mine. Of course, Almarian crystal is superior to any other crystal. It wouldn't break!"

"I don't know about you," Jane told Allegra. "I'm afraid we three are failing completely at our queening lessons. Queening is supposed to be serious business, and I don't see any signs that you're any more serious today than you were the first day we arrived."

"Don't worry," Allegra assured the roommates. "I may not be any more serious, but I'm learning a lot from you — just like I did from the first day I set foot on the campus of Canby Hall. You can't imagine how good you are for me. Especially if you keep Armand out of our hair!"

"Deal," Jane said.

Just then, Fenster knocked at the door of the suite. "Your Royal Highness," he said, addressing Allegra, the same princess who had just nearly begun a pillow fight. "Her Majesty informs me that Your Highness's presence is requested in the seamstress's studio."

"Thanks, Fenster," Allegra said, standing up. "That means final fitting time. I'll see you tonight. It's going to be another stuffy party. I just wish Andy were going to dance. That would be so nice, wouldn't it be?" she asked wistfully. With that, she left the suite.

"Every time we turn around, we've got another problem on our hands, don't we?" Toby asked.

"Nothing we can't handle," Jane said bravely, trying to believe it. But the fact was, it was becoming clearer and clearer that both Armand and Andy could be big trouble.

"Wonder if Parrish McCoy could make it here by tomorrow," Toby mused.

It was all Jane could do to resist throwing another silk-covered pillow at Toby. But Toby was next to a Montavian lamp, and it wasn't clear that the Montavian artifact was as durable as the Almarian one.

CHAPTER TWELVE

Jane and Toby slipped into the pew of the palace chapel where the wedding was to take place. The rehearsal was going full tilt, and it was fascinating to watch.

The bishop stood up at the front of the chapel. Allegra and James were in front of him, and the bridal party, including both kings and queens, was carefully arranged around the chancel. The entire ceremony was being orchestrated by the joint chiefs of protocol from Almare and Montavia — who most certainly did not always agree on the proper way to do things.

Every time the Almarian protocol expert won an argument, Armand smirked.

"I guess this stuff is pretty important," Toby said in awe.

"You really think it matters which of the mothers is escorted to the chancel first?" Jane asked.

"They've certainly argued about it long enough," Toby said.

"That just shows you how much it *doesn't* matter," Jane explained. "If it were really important, everybody would know the answer."

"No! No! *No!*" One of the protocol experts was yelping. "If Her Highness does as you have requested, the soles of Her Highness's shoes will be revealed to the public!"

"Give me a break," Toby said. "And remind me, if I should ever be foolish enough to fall in love and want to get married, that Rev. Barker in Rattlesnake Creek does a nice little ten-minute ceremony. No fuss, no bother."

"And then Parrish McCoy arrives?"

"No, Parrish McCoy comes to the service. He's the organist at the church — except when the organ breaks, or if there's a power outage or something, in which case Parrish plays the fiddle at the services."

Jane pulled back to look at her friend, wondering for a brief moment if she were kidding. But the look on Toby's face told Jane that she was telling the truth. And at that moment, in the middle of the rehearsal for a very complicated ceremony, with every inch of it being argued out by two people whose only concerns were winning arguments, Jane thought Toby had a point. There was a lot to be said for Rattlesnake Creek.

"Hey, did you see that?" Toby said, nudging Jane out of her Texas reverie.

"No, what?"

"It's Armand. He's up to something."

Jane watched carefully. Armand stood near his brother, uneasily. He shifted his weight from one foot to the other and then stuck his hands in his pockets. His mother flashed a warning look at him. His hands came out of his pockets. In his right hand was a piece of paper. Armand glanced at it and then shoved it back into his pocket.

"*That,*" Toby hissed. "He was looking at that before."

"What's the matter with looking at a piece of paper?" Jane asked.

"Nothing, usually. By the *way* he was looking at it, though, he had 'guilt' written all over his face."

At that point, anything Armand was doing became overshadowed by the misbehavior of three of the flower girls who started batting one another with their mock baskets of flowers. The young boys who were paired with them joined in the melée and before anybody could stop it, six little kids were rolling on the floor punching one another. At the chancel, the rest of the wedding party watched, horrified.

"Does this kind of thing go on in Rattlesnake Creek?" Jane whispered to Toby.

"All the time," Toby said, nodding. "Now I feel right at home."

That started Jane giggling. She tried to

hide her laughter, but Toby started laughing, too. They covered their mouths with their hands and did the best they could — until Andy spotted them. When Andy's eyes met Jane's and Toby's, it was all over. Andy issued a most unladylike snort, and then burst into laughter, watching one very properly dressed six-year-old boy deliver a roundhouse punch to the little girl next to him. Finally, almost everybody in the wedding party was able to see how funny the children were being and everybody joined in the laughter — except Armand.

While Jane and Toby were still giggling, they noticed him once again reaching in his pocket for the paper.

What could it be? Jane asked herself. She didn't know, but she had a bad feeling about it. She had made Allegra a promise, and she wanted to keep it. It would be one thing if a fist fight broke out among the flower girls and ring bearers at a royal wedding. People could laugh about that for generations. But a determined Armand could cause *real* trouble.

She just *had* to find out what was on that piece of paper!

The first chance Jane had to get near Armand was at the rehearsal dinner, another formal dinner dance at the Montavian palace. This time, Allegra and James were seated with their parents at the head table, and the roommates were seated with their escorts at a separate table.

Andy and Ramad were in a world of their own. Jane and Toby knew it was up to them to figure out what Armand's scheme was — and to stop him.

The first course of the dinner was pâté de foie gras with truffles.

"This is just delicious," Jane remarked. "Reminds me of school."

Toby burst into laughter.

"Didn't you tell me the food at school was awful?" André asked her.

"Absolutely," she assured him.

He turned to Jane. "So how does this delicious pâté remind you of school?" he asked.

"It's the same color as the tuna fish casserole," she explained.

He looked at her uncertainly. "It's true," Toby assured him.

"I hope there are good restaurants around," he said.

"Oh, sure. There's Pizza Pete's and the Greaf — it was called The Greenleaf Cafe, but a lot of letters fell out of the sign, so we just call it The Greaf, from what's left of the letters — and the — "

"Spare us," Armand said. He had reacquired his superior tone, and Jane knew that he meant it when he asked to be spared.

"Only if you'll dance with me," Jane teased him.

He pursed his lips as if the idea were very distasteful, and then he grudgingly stood up and led her to the dance floor.

When the music began, Armand put his right arm around her waist and took her right hand in his left. He began shuffling her around the dance floor in an uninspired foxtrot. If this was Almarian dancing, Jane didn't want any part of it, but then she already knew she didn't want any part of Armand. However, Jane knew this was her chance so she gritted her teeth and began. "The rehearsal was so interesting today."

"It was a bore," he responded.

"Weren't the children funny?" she asked.

"The children were misbehaving," he corrected her.

"The ceremony will be so wonderful tomorrow," she said.

"The ceremony will be as boring as the rehearsal," he told her.

Jane was ready to give up. Making small talk with a snob like Armand was just about impossible. So far, all she'd learned was that everything was boring.

Hey, wait a minute, she told herself. If the ceremony is going to be a bore, then that means that whatever awful thing he's going to do will not be at the ceremony. He'd never think something bad he was going to do would be boring. He thinks much too much of himself for that.

"What about the reception?" she asked. "Will that be boring, too?"

"What makes you ask that?" he retorted suspiciously.

Bingo! she said to herself. At least she could relax through the ceremony.

"Why do you ask that?" he repeated, and Jane realized that she was getting too close to something. She had to change the subject.

"Tell me, Armand," she said, pretending to ignore his question. "I noticed a landscape painting on the wall in the Almarian ballroom. . . ."

That did it. Armand had an opinion about the painting and about the painter and about his choice of subject. He expressed his opinion for the remainder of the dance and Jane didn't have to listen to a word of it.

"Did you get anything?" Toby asked her a few minutes later in the women's room while they were freshening their makeup.

"Nothing about the paper, but whatever it is, I'm pretty sure it doesn't have anything to do with the ceremony — just with the reception. But the minute I asked him about that, he got suspicious, so I changed the subject."

"How do you just go and switch subjects on a prince?" Toby asked.

"With Armand, it's easy. You change the subject to him or to Almare — preferably him. He *always* goes along with that."

"All right, I'll give it a try," Toby told her. "I clued André in on the problem. He'll ask you to dance, so if I've got my social rules straight, Armand will *have* to ask me to dance, right?"

"That's the way I learned it in dancing school," Jane assured her. "But, of course, that was just *Boston*. Now, in *Almare*. . . ."

They emerged from the powder room laughing together, and as promised, when they returned to the table, André asked Armand if he might dance with Jane. Armand granted permission and immediately asked if he might dance with Toby. Everybody agreed very politely.

"Watch out for your toes," Jane hissed at Toby as they headed for the dance floor. "He's got a wicked right."

Toby smiled sweetly.

"Why Armand," Toby cooed when they started dancing. "It's such fun to dance with you! Back home in Rattlesnake Creek, all we ever do is square dance. You can teach me so much!"

"And you have so much to learn!" he responded.

Toby felt they'd gotten off on the wrong foot, so to speak. She tried to redirect the conversation. "Tell me about tomorrow," she began.

"It's the wedding," he said, as if she didn't know that.

"Well, I know all about the wedding. I was at the rehearsal today, so I know what to expect then. But what happens afterward?" she asked. "At the wedding breakfast and reception."

"It's just another party," he said. "Probably as boring as this one — for the most part, that is."

"Anything special going to happen? Anything I should know about?"

"Probably not," he said. Then he stepped on her left foot with his right — just as Jane had promised. It was all Toby could do to keep from grimacing — something she was sure a proper young Almarian lady would never do.

She hadn't gotten much information from him, but she had to agree with Jane that it sounded like trouble would break at the reception rather than at the wedding. Using Jane's technique, she asked Armand about the employment situation in Almare and while he droned on, she decided it was time to see if Andy could get anything out of him.

As soon as she returned to the table, she proposed that Andy and Jane join her in the women's room.

"The American makeup industry leaves much to be desired," Armand remarked as the three of them departed.

Since Andy had had so little time to dress for the dance, following the wedding rehearsal, Toby and Jane hadn't even had a chance to fill her in. Now, they had only a few precious minutes.

Toby began. "We're sure Armand is up to something, and we've got to stop him."

"We need your help," Jane said urgently.

"Oh, sure," Andy replied dreamily, and continued gazing almost blankly while Jane told her what was up.

"Have you heard a word I said?" Jane asked, realizing that the dreamy look hadn't left Andy's face.

"Oh, I'm sorry, Jane. My mind was someplace else."

"Obviously," Jane said sharply. "But before I repeat myself, tell me what's so important that you can't listen to me."

"It's Ramad," she said.

Jane and Toby exchanged looks that said this was what they were expecting, but when Andy continued, they realized it was much *more* than they were expecting.

"He's invited me to come visit his country. He wants me to meet his family — and maybe he's thinking about an engagement."

"He's *what*?" Toby and Jane asked in a single, astonished voice.

"I think he wants me to marry him and stay there," Andy repeated in a whisper. Then she delivered her bombshell. "And I may just do it, too."

Jane and Toby knew right away that not only would Andy be no help with Armand, but she could very well be a major problem herself.

"It's moments like this that make me wish we were back at Canby Hall," Toby said. "Tuna casserole and all."

"I know what you mean," Jane said.

CHAPTER THIRTEEN

When the girls awakened and looked out the window of their suite, they saw a very big crowd gathered around the palace in honor of their friend, Allegra, and her bridegroom.

The chapel held less than a thousand people, but it seemed that the entire populations of both Montavia and Almare surrounded the palace — and it was clear from the television cameras and equipment trucks that everybody in the world who wasn't there was watching events unfold on television.

"This is the hottest ticket in town!" Jane whispered to Toby as they were escorted to their seats in the chapel by André, later that morning.

"Everybody loves royalty," André agreed, "not to mention a wedding." Since they had talked about exactly that subject with their friend Andy, far into the night, they were extremely aware of it. The girls exchanged glances and then, having arrived at their assigned seats in the chapel, entered the pews and sat quietly, each with her own uncomfortable thoughts on the subject of Andy.

The wedding began at ten o'clock sharp. It began with the appearance of six chastened children. All of the flower girls and ringbearers walked down the aisle as if they knew that a wrong step would bring disaster. It was clear that there would be no brawls this morning — no roundhouse punches, no bloody noses. Jane suppressed a smile, remembering the fight at the rehearsal. Somehow, the fight seemed a little more natural than the children's cautious march at the ceremony.

The bridesmaids came after the children. There were six of them, but one of them was far more beautiful than the others — in Jane's opinion — and that was her friend, Andrea Cord. Jane and Toby nearly gasped with delight when Andy appeared at the door of the chapel. The only other time they'd seen Andy in her bridesmaid's dress was in Room 407 of Baker House at Canby Hall. That seemed like a very long time ago, and the girl who walked down the aisle a mere four weeks later seemed like a very different one. After all, back at school, Andy had never *heard* of such a person as Prince

Ramad — much less fallen in love with him.

"She *still* looks like a fairy godperson," Toby whispered, reminding Jane of Andy's words the day the dress had arrived.

"Yes, and a beautiful one, too."

They were both extremely proud of their friend and very glad to be with her. If only they didn't have to worry about her as well. And about Armand.

Jane pushed her worries aside and concentrated on the very special event which was unfolding in front of her.

Finally, Princess Allegra of Montavia appeared at the door of the chapel, escorted by her father, King Rudolph. The congregation, which had remained seated during the arrival of the wedding party, stood up to honor the king and princess.

The girls had seen Allegra many times in the previous week and many times at Canby Hall. It had always surprised them to find that, though she was a princess, she was truly just another person. Now, looking at her in yards and yards of white silk and lace, it was surprising to see that this person was truly a princess, truly regal. And as she passed them, she looked in their direction and winked. So, not only was she a princess, but a happy one, too. Allegra seemed to understand, in a way that was hard for them, that this pomp and circumstance, the ceremony and the ritual, was important, but underneath, one person was about to be married to another and that was much more important than yards of lace or jewel-studded crowns.

The congregation was seated and the ceremony began.

In many ways, it was much like every other wedding that had ever taken place (except maybe in Rattlesnake Creek, Jane thought wryly). Jane even felt a tear of joy come to her eye when she heard Allegra say, "I, Allegra, take thee, James . . ." But Jane always cried just a little bit at weddings.

After the marriage part of the ceremony, came the coronation part. Allegra and James were each made a crown prince/princess of the other's country by Royal Decree of their kings. Then the kings made more Royal Decrees about the union of the countries which wouldn't actually become official until Allegra and James became king and queen of both countries. There were many whereases and heretofores and henceforths, but the fact was that that part of the ceremony was kind of boring.

Then, once rings and crowns had been exchanged, and signatures had been inscribed in dusty old volumes, the bishop took over again, and the religious service concluded the ceremony. A boys' choir sang two lovely pieces, and the bishop delivered a brief homily — not very different from the one the minister in Rattlesnake Creek gave at weddings, Toby thought. Then, the bishop gave permission for the crown prince to kiss the crown princess.

James turned to Allegra and slowly lifted the lacy veil which had covered her face during the ceremony and the two of them sealed their solemn vows with a tender kiss. Jane felt a lump rise in her throat. She dabbed at the tears forming in her eyes. Next to her, Toby was grinning. It was impossible not to be touched by such a lovely moment.

Then came Andy's big part. Allegra and James turned and linked arms for their recessional march. Andy handed her own bouquet to one of the little girls and hastened to Allegra. Her job was to readjust the long train on Allegra's dress so it would flow smoothly behind her. Andy did the job quickly and efficiently, retrieved her bouquet, and returned to her assigned spot.

The music began and the royal couple marched proudly and happily out of the chapel to be received by the cheering crowds of Montavians and Almarians who awaited them outside.

The rest of the wedding party followed. First Armand, escorting André's sister, Katerina. The prince had a mean look of distaste on his face. That made Jane very nervous. Armand was followed by Ramad and Andy, walking together. When Andy reached the place where Jane and Toby were sitting, her eyes darted over to meet theirs and she winked at them. *That* made Jane even more nervous. It reminded her too much of the wink that Allegra had delivered on her way to getting married.

"Well," Jane said to Toby as the rest of the crowd began to file out of the chapel. "Whatever might happen at the wedding breakfast, or *later*," her words were heavy with meaning, and Jane knew Toby understood she was talking about Andy and Ramad, "at least the wedding itself went off without a hitch. It was *beautiful*, wasn't it?"

"It sure was," Toby agreed. "Couldn't have done it better in Rattlesnake Creek!"

When they emerged from the chapel, the girls were reunited with Armand and André. They were to ride to the wedding breakfast with Armand and André in the limousine. Jane and Toby joined them at the car and climbed in. There were two seats, facing each other in the gigantic car. Jane and Armand were seated facing forward. Toby and André rode with their backs to the driver.

"Golly, I never saw anything like that ceremony!" Toby said in awe as the car eased its way through the crowd. "You guys were terrific, too. No mistakes at all!"

"Oh, perhaps just one," Armand said pointedly, reminding everybody of his own feelings about the marriage of his brother, and his country.

Toby was too enthusiastic about the experience to let Armand's sour tone dampen her feelings. She continued talking, mostly to André about how impressive it was. Jane was quiet, paying little attention to her.

She noticed that Armand wasn't paying any attention to Toby, either. In fact, she noticed that, once again, he was paying attention to a piece of paper. Armand removed a sheet of paper, folded in thirds, from his jacket pocket. While Toby and André chatted happily about the wedding, Armand unfolded the paper to glance at it. Jane pretended to be listening intently to the conversation and even leaned forward to assure Armand she was involved in it, but her eyes never left the paper because she was sure that was the heart of her trouble. She waited for the opportunity she was sure would come.

Then it arrived. The car swung around a sharp corner to the left. Jane pretended she lost her balance and was thrown to the right in the backseat. Armand, fending her off, dropped his precious paper to the floor of the car. As soon as he could, he grabbed for it, but Jane got it first, read as much as she could, appearing not to notice at all, and handed it back to him.

For the remainder of the trip, Jane was completely silent. What she had seen on Armand's precious piece of paper was the "Best Man's Toast," to be delivered at the wedding breakfast. The opening words were enough to confirm her worst suspicions. It began, "You may be surprised, but there is something I want to share with you this morning. Today is a dark day for the kingdom of Almare." If Armand delivered that toast, the entire wedding would be ruined. Although his words could not break the marriage, nor could they undo the union of the countries which had been formalized at the wedding, they *could* create such bad feelings between the two kingdoms that the effect would be devastating all the same. Somehow, Jane had to stop him from delivering the toast.

But how?

As soon as they arrived at the palace, Jane summoned Toby and Andy and explained the situation. The girls both understood the seriousness of it at once. Armand had to be stopped at all costs.

"How about we lock him in a closet?" Toby suggested.

"I don't really think that's practical," Jane told her woefully, though the idea had a lot to be said for it, including the fact that she could then spend the rest of the day without him.

"Can you steal the paper?" Andy asked.

"I probably could," Jane admitted, "though I don't have much experience in picking pockets, but the fact is he's looked at it so much he probably has the whole darn thing memorized by now anyway."

"One time a cowboy I know went to Mexico and ate peppers so hot they burned his tongue and he couldn't talk for hours. Can we do something along that line?" Toby said.

"I don't think there are any Mexican dishes on the breakfast menu," Jane said.

"I think I know how to handle this," Andy said. "But it's going to take split-second timing — and a lot of help. Come on, we don't have a minute to waste!"

Then Andy shared her plan with Toby and Jane and they all agreed it might, just *might*, work.

CHAPTER FOURTEEN

The next few minutes were very busy ones for the Canby girls. Andy had to get something from her closet. Jane was assigned to talk to Fenster, and Toby was given the task of explaining the situation to the orchestra leader.

Fifteen minutes later, they met at the wedding breakfast and exchanged nods and winks. Nobody seemed to notice that Andy was walking a little differently. Everybody seemed to have eyes only for the royal couple — everybody that was, except the roommates, who did not take their eyes off Armand. Armand was too involved with himself, as usual, to notice the attention he was garnering from the American girls, and that was a good thing.

The ballroom was set up with tables around the dance floor. The Royal Protocol Schedule called for "Champagne Breakfast followed by the Dance." That meant that when the champagne was served, there would be formal toasts. That's where the girls' plan was going to irrevocably change the Royal Protocol Schedule at least a little bit — for the good.

When the champagne was served to the head table, consisting of Allegra, James, and their parents, the toasts began.

First, King Rudolph rose and gave a speech welcoming James to their family and welcoming Almare to their kingdom. Next to her, Jane could almost feel Armand shudder. Then, Armand and James's father rose and gave a toast. Next, it was James's turn. The girls barely heard his words, knowing that, as soon as James sat down, Armand would rise for his toast.

Andy slid out of her seat and hurried to the small room nearby to change clothes. It was a terrible breach of etiquette to leave the room when the Crown Prince was speaking, but everybody knew she was an American and, therefore, probably ignorant of such things. As the guests rose to join James in his toast to his bride, Andy slipped back inside, to the edge of the dance floor.

She watched carefully. The guests applauded James's toast and then everybody sat down. Everybody that is, except Armand. The crowd turned to him expectantly. It was almost time.

"Ahem," he said, silencing the guests.

"You may be surprised," he began slowly and deliberately, "but there is something I want to share with you this morning."

At that instant, before Armand could utter another word, Andy nodded to the orchestra conductor, who raised his baton, and with the downbeat began the music to Juliet's solo in the ballet of *Romeo and Juliet*.

Andy swept onto the dance floor and began the performance of her life.

She'd never danced the piece to live music and it seemed to inspire her in a way she could not have imagined. She felt she *became* the young girl, Juliet, so deeply and hopelessly in love with Romeo — the one man whose love was forbidden to her.

As the music rose to its crescendoes, Andy was drawn further and further into the part. Her audience disappeared and her whole being was concentrated on the steps she knew so well. When she leapt, she could feel her body spring from the floor as never before. She executed her arabesques and pirouettes perfectly according to the intricate choreography of the piece and when, as the final notes died away, she lay on the floor, a young Juliet, dying for love, the applause of the hundreds of guests at the wedding breakfast told her that she had succeeded well beyond her own expectations — and even hopes.

"Brava!" came the shout from James, who stood to honor her. Immediately, Allegra stood up, and they were joined by the kings and queens of Almare and Montavia. Then, all of the guests stood up to applaud.

Andy could barely breathe, she was so filled with the excitement of it all. She'd danced in public before, but it had never been like this. It was wonderful — more than she could ever have imagined.

She rose gracefully and turned to the royal couple. She then curtseyed so low that her forehead nearly touched the floor. When she rose, the applause burst out again.

It was only then that Andy allowed her eyes to turn to the thwarted Armand. He was standing next to Jane, his face flushed with fury. It was *exactly* what the girls had hoped for.

Andy returned to the entrance of the room. When the applause finally died away, James spoke again.

"Armand," he said, addressing his brother. "You promised us a surprise, and I must say, you have delivered one. On this day, you have honored us in a way we could not have anticipated. We thank you, from the bottoms of our hearts, for providing this very special performance by our friend, the talented American dancer, Andrea Cord. Thanks to you both."

The guests then began applauding Armand for his wonderful "surprise." Under the circumstances, there was no way, no way at all, that Armand could ever deliver his poisonous "toast." He glared at Jane, Toby, and over to Andy. They smiled back sweetly — as if nothing unusual had happened at all. Andy then slipped out of the room to quickly freshen up and change back into her bridesmaid's dress.

Then breakfast was served. Jane lifted a bite of the fresh fruit salad with her fruit salad fork and turned to her escort. "Say, Armand," Jane began innocently. "You know, you and I were talking the other day about some of the really neat traditions at American weddings, remember?"

"I remember," he said glumly.

"How did you like the one about the tin cans on the 'getaway car'?" Jane asked. "You know, sometimes people take shaving cream and write on the car, too. Nothing mean, of course, things like 'Just Married.' "

"Really?" Armand asked, suddenly interested in crass American customs. He took a few bites of his own appetizer. "Shaving cream, you say?"

"Sure, the aerosol kind. You have that in Almare, don't you?" Jane asked innocently.

Armand nodded idly. "Tin cans?"

"Sure, you tie them together and then tie them to the fender of the car. Makes a big racket," she explained. "It can be really embarrassing, too."

"Hmmmm," he said, so engrossed in his

own thoughts that he dropped a piece of pineapple on his lap.

When the Eggs Benedict was served, Armand took only a few bites and then excused himself from the table.

The girls had to stifle their giggles until they were sure he couldn't hear them.

"Where has Armand gone to?" André asked Toby, confused by the laughter.

"If we've figured him right — and so far today, we *seem* to have his number — he's gone in search of shaving cream and tin cans."

"He's what?" Ramad asked.

"He thinks he's going to decorate the car Allegra and James will leave in for their honeymoon with shaving cream and tin cans," Andy told him.

"Oh, but that will be a terrible embarrassment for James and Allegra," André protested. "What have you three girls done?"

"Decoy car," Toby said.

"What we've done," Jane explained "is to have good old Fenster put a decoy car out in front of the palace. Armand is welcome to decorate that to his heart's content. The minute he's finished his handiwork, Fenster will remove that one, to the royal carwash, presumably, and replace it with the actual car James and Allegra are using. And, in the meantime, we are completely free of Armand."

"Oh, my!" Ramad said, in frank admiration. "You three are really quite a team, if you can pull that off."

"Yes," Jane agreed. "We *are* quite a team." She grinned broadly at her friends, proud of what they had accomplished together.

Andy was still glowing from the success of her solo performance as Juliet long after the last bit of her wedding breakfast was gone. All during the meal, wedding guests came to congratulate her — even King Rudolph. But most important to her was when Allegra and James came to thank her. Andy shuddered to think she'd almost let the opportunity pass, because of Ramad.

Andy glanced at him as he sat next to her now. He looked very serious, as he had two nights before when her friends had asked him about his country and its customs. Andy wondered what he was thinking. He was probably concerned, as she was, about the fact that in another day, they would all be leaving Montavia. What would the future bring? In sharp contrast to the joy she felt about her performance, she felt quite confused about the future.

"Andrea, would you care to take a walk with me?" he asked. She nodded.

"I have to change my shoes, though — I still have on my toe shoes, and I can't really walk very well in them. You can help me," she said.

Together, they walked from the ballroom to the foyer, where Fenster had stowed her pumps. She sat on a needlepoint-covered antique Montavian chair while Ramad unfastened the satin ribbons of her toe shoes.

"I feel sort of like Cinderella," she remarked.

"Oh, in the fairy tale," he said, recognizing the story. "It has a happy ending, doesn't it?"

"Of course," Andy told him. "All fairy tales have happy endings. The prince and princess always live happily ever after."

"If only that were real life," he said, slipping her regular shoes onto her feet. He offered her a hand and she took it, standing up next to him. Although he'd originally suggested a walk, it wasn't really very practical considering the full gown Andy was wearing. They walked along the narrow hallway on the main floor until they found a room where they could sit and talk in private. It was a library, walls covered with leather-covered books, and furnished with leather-covered sofas.

"What a lovely place," Andy declared, sitting on one of the soft sofas. Ramad sat next to her and took her hand.

"Andrea," he began. "I've never known anyone like you before. I have never met a person who had such determination and such talent. You nearly took my breath away when you danced today. It was as fine a performance as I've ever seen. I mean that."

Andy was very pleased with Ramad's compliment, but from his seriousness, she had the feeling she wasn't going to like what he was going to say to her.

"There is something I must tell you, though. In my country, you will not be able to dance. It is our tradition that only men dance. In fact, women are rarely seen in public — and never without their husbands. They do not speak unless spoken to, and they never speak to another man. When they are with their women friends, they may do as they wish — as long as it is in private."

"You're kidding!" Andy said. "Why that sounds like the dark ages, Ramad!"

"It must seem that way to you," he said. "But you see, a woman is a flower which has blossomed for her husband's pleasure."

"Do you really believe that?" Andy asked, astonished.

"To tell you the truth, Andrea, I believed it up until the moment I met you. I used to scorn all the things I read about American women — women's liberation and such. Now I think I understand it better. You have opened my eyes."

"You don't expect to treat your wife that way, do you?" Andy said, suddenly realizing the gravity of his words — and what they meant to her.

"Traditions run very deep," he said. "My people will expect me to hold to our traditions. Oh, I may be able to change some of them, but I can't ask my people to accept a king who does not live the lives they do, who does not believe as they do. Yes, Andrea, I will treat my wife as a flower who blossoms only for me — and she will behave accordingly."

Andy stared at the hand that held hers. "That's not me, Ramad," she said, deep regret in her voice.

"I know," he told her. "For a while, I hoped, Andrea. I truly hoped. But then I realized that bringing you to my country would be terribly unfair to *you*, as well as to my people."

She tried to withdraw her hand from his, but he held it tightly.

"Don't pull away from me," he said softly. "For I love you, and I think you feel the same way about me."

"I've never felt this way about anybody, Ramad. But you're right. Your country is no place for someone like me. While you and I were walking, picnicking, and skiing together, it seemed just fine to me to give up my dancing. I knew, deep inside, that that was the price I would have to pay for your love. But today, when I danced, I understood, as I've always known in my heart, that dance *is* the most important thing in the world to me."

"I knew that the moment I saw you take the floor — and I can't ask you to give that up for me. This prince isn't living in a fairy tale and I won't live happily ever after, because I won't be with you."

Andy sat silently for a while, hoping she wouldn't cry. She gazed around at the books which covered all of the walls. It seemed that all the wisdom in the world, in all the books in the world, couldn't have prepared her for this moment.

"You want me to tell you I'll give up dance for you, don't you?" she asked.

"I hoped — " he began.

"I know." She nodded. "But it isn't just dance I'd be giving up, Ramad. It's *me*. I can't be the kind of person you need. I have to be myself. I have to be able to say what's on my mind, go where I want to go, think for myself. I guess this time Cinderella doesn't get the prince. That doesn't mean the fairy tale is over — it just means it will have to have a different ending."

"You have such a wonderful way of looking at things," Ramad said, smiling at her. "That means your prince is still waiting for his princess. Well, my parents probably have chosen her already, but that won't mean I can't be friends, outside of my own land, with a wonderful girl like yourself."

"That could be fun," Andy said, considering the possibilities. "So when are you coming to America?"

"Actually, I have applied to the School of Government in Cambridge, Massachusetts.

Is that anywhere near your Canby Hall?"

"Just a half-hour train ride away!" Andy said excitedly.

"Then perhaps I shall have the opportunity to try this tuna fish casserole you girls have been talking about so much," Ramad said.

Andy burst into laughter. She could barely picture her handsome prince eating in the school dining room. "No way!" she said. "We'll dine at Pizza Pete's instead!"

"All right," he said. "It's a date and a promise. Shall we seal the promise with a kiss?"

Andy couldn't say no, and she didn't want to. He touched her chin with his hand and raised her face until his lips met hers. The promise was made, and they both knew it was right.

CHAPTER FIFTEEN

"Hey, where have you been?" Jane said as Andy walked into Allegra's suite. Toby looked on from the chair next to Jane's.

"I was talking with Ramad in the library," she explained. "Fenster found me and told me you wanted me here, Allegra."

"I do," Allegra said. "I'm up here to change out of my gown, and James and I are going to be leaving for our wedding trip in about an hour. I haven't had nearly enough time to visit with any of you three, but especially you, Andy, so I thought we could visit while I change." Allegra's maid was carefully undoing the buttons on her dress. Her going-away outfit was laid out for her. It was an elegant suit, dark blue linen, with a yellow blouse. "The Almarian colors," Allegra told the girls. Then, for a moment, she disappeared under the yards of silk and lace as her maid lifted her wedding gown over her head.

"It's been wonderful having you here," Allegra began.

"It's been wonderful *being* here," Jane protested.

"Even with Armand?" Allegra asked suspiciously.

"Maybe even especially with Armand," Jane said. "He really provided a challenge to us — and a lot of fun in the end."

"What was all that business about his toast and your dance, Andy?" she asked. "I knew there was something suspicious going on there, but I couldn't figure it out. All I could see was that Armand was furious at you."

"Oh, and he had a right to be," Jane assured her. "We really fixed him good then!"

"But what *was* it?" Allegra asked. "Is this one of those things I'm going to be better off not knowing?"

"That's a good way to put it," Jane said.

Allegra slipped her arms into her blouse. "Want to hear something astonishing about Armand?" she said tantalizingly.

"Nothing would astonish me about Armand," Jane assured her. "Nothing short of his entering a hog-calling contest, I mean."

"Well, this isn't actually about Armand. It's about André's sister, Katerina. You met her, didn't you, Toby?"

Toby recalled André's shy younger sister. She'd been at the stables when they had gone riding. "Sure," she said to her friends. "She's the pretty blonde kid who was sitting at the table next to ours at the disco party." Jane and Andy recalled seeing her there. "And she's the bridesmaid that Armand escorted out of the chapel. Remember?" They nodded.

"Well, it turns out that Katerina is just madly in love with Armand. She's had a crush on him for years."

"Ugh," Jane remarked. "She can have him."

"Good idea."

"Enough gossip," Allegra said. She pulled her skirt down over her head and smoothed it with her hands while the maid did the hook and zipper. As soon as that was done, Allegra sat down at her vanity and her hairdresser appeared from nowhere to re-fashion her coiffure in a manner more suitable for travel. "What I really wanted to do was to thank you all for being such a help to me."

"You keep saying that," Andy told her, "but I don't see how we've helped you at all. You don't want to drain any swamps or let any peasants out of the dungeons. We can't talk you into diplomatic relations with anybody. Exactly what good *have* we done you?" Andy asked.

"You silly girls!" Allegra exclaimed. "You

think that all there is to queening is knowing something about history. Well, anybody in the world can learn about history. *Even* a princess! That's the easy part. What you three have given me is far more important, and elusive, than book learning. You've given me friendship. You've shown me what loyalty without strings really means. *That's* the part of 'queening' that I can't get from a book. That's why I wanted you here and that's why I'm glad you came — not even counting the laughs we've had, *and* your fabulous performance, Andy."

"Oh," Andy said. "I see. Sometimes, for some people, it's very hard to see how the rest of the world lives, isn't it?"

Andy's friends looked at her to see if that question had some special meaning for her, but her face revealed nothing to them.

"Yes, Andy, it is. And you'll remember, when we first met at Canby Hall, the thing you and I had in common was that we both wanted to be judged for what we were, not for what other people expected us to be. You have been good at reminding me about that. And you've been good at judging me for what I am. So thank you. All of you. Now, that's enough seriousness. Let's get on with the fun. Tell me another American tradition about weddings."

"Well, there's the throwing of the bridal bouquet," Jane said.

"What's that about?" Allegra asked.

"Just before you climb into the car, you toss your bouquet to all the unmarried women — and whichever one catches it is going to be the next one to get married."

"I like that!" Allegra said. They were about to tell her about throwing rice, and the new trend toward throwing birdseed because it had been discovered the rice was harmful to birds, when there was a knock at the door. It was Allegra's mother, coming to help her with the final preparations for her departure. This was clearly a mother-daughter time. The roommates excused themselves to return to the party.

The girls found Armand strutting around at the party smugly. That had to mean that he'd finished decorating the car and was feeling terribly proud of himself. André was standing nearby with his sister, Katerina. Armed with their new knowledge about André's sister, they could easily see how her eyes kept wandering over to Armand in an otherwise inexplicably dreamy fashion.

"Let's get into the cupid business," Jane said. "I can't wait to see how Armand reacts to somebody who actually *likes* him."

Toby and Andy joined André and Katerina. Jane fetched Armand and brought him over to the circle where her friends were standing.

"Armand, you know André's sister, Katerina, don't you?" Jane said smoothly.

Armand clicked his heels together in acknowledgment. Katerina blushed deeply, her eyes glued to the ground. "Why, André," Armand said. "Where have you been keeping your lovely sister all this time?"

André looked at Armand with surprise. "I thought you had met before," André protested. "Katerina has been at school in Almare for four years now."

"Almare?" he asked in surprise. "You like my country, then?"

"Oh, yes!" she breathed. "Very much, indeed!"

"Would you like to dance?" Armand asked Katerina.

"Oh, yes!" she said again. Armand led her onto the dance floor and as the music began, he stepped on her left foot. She smiled reassuringly at him.

The roommates burst into giggles.

"What's so funny?" Ramad asked, joining them.

"I think Cinderella just met the prince of her dreams," Jane told him. "Trouble is, he may crush the glass slipper. See, he's not much of a dancer!"

Andy winced. It made her uncomfortable for Jane to talk about fairy tales so soon after her own had been shattered, but Jane had no way of knowing about that at all. Ramad didn't seem to notice, or if he did, he didn't let it bother him. "Dance with me,

Andy? I promise not to shatter any more glass slippers today."

She smiled and joined him on the dance floor.

Toby and Jane practically collapsed at their table, completely exhausted from all the planning and plotting they'd done so far in the day. Now if only they could figure out what was going on with Andy and Ramad.

"I know something isn't right, but I can't figure it," Jane said.

"She's a big girl, Jane," Toby reminded her. "Whether or not she makes a mistake, she'll make it whatever we do."

"You're a real comfort," Jane snapped.

"That's not what I'm trying to be. I'm trying to be a realist."

"Well, you're that, too."

They watched the dancers in silence for a few minutes, until the orchestra stopped and played a fanfare. That could only mean that it was time for Allegra and James to leave, and the guests were being invited to see them off — in their *un*decorated car.

The guests all collected at the front door to the palace to toss rose petals at the crown prince and princess as they left for their wedding trip. Jane, Andy, and Toby stood near one another, close to the foot of the stairs where the couple would appear.

Allegra and James came down the stairs together and the shower of rose petals began. The sweet scent of the flowers permeated the air and the lovely rainbow of colors made a gala scene. Just before Allegra came to the foot of the stairs, she paused, her bouquet in her hand.

"A fine old American custom!" she announced, and tossed her bouquet in a lazy arc straight into Andy's arms.

Jane and Toby gasped. Could it be true? The look of surprise on Andy's face was genuine.

"No way!" Andy announced. "Not me and not *now*! Let sombody else have the pleasure!" With that, she tossed the bouquet again, this time very carefully aimed — at none other than Katerina. The shy girl caught it and grinned slyly to herself.

The roommates laughed with joy. Wait until Armand learned about *that* old American custom!

CHAPTER SIXTEEN

A few hours later, Jane, Toby, and Andy were on their way home. They settled into their compartment on the train to Amsterdam. It was hard to believe that all the wonderful glamour and excitement of the wedding was over and that they would actually be back at Canby Hall — land of the brown tuna fish casserole — the next day.

"I think I could learn to love palace life," Jane said.

"Maybe," Andy said. "But there are real drawbacks to it, too."

"Like what?" Jane asked in surprise. "And does this have anything to do with a certain crown prince and a certain bridal bouquet which was *not* caught by a certain American Cinderella?"

Andy grinned sheepishly. "Yeah," she confessed.

"So tell!" Jane urged her.

Andy told her friends about her conversation with Ramad in the library. They were a little sad that Andy's fairy tale romance hadn't come true, but they were even more relieved that their friend had made a wise decision to stay at school and stick with her ballet.

"What an experience it was for you, though," Jane said. "Not everybody gets to fall in love with a prince!"

"And for everybody who doesn't fall in love with a prince, you've got somebody who doesn't have to go through the pain of falling *out* of love with him, either. It's not easy — and it's especially not going to be easy when he goes to school in Cambridge."

"Cambridge? You mean like near Boston, like thirty miles from Canby Hall?"

"Same place," Andy assured her. "He's planning to study there. Can you picture Prince Ramad at Pizza Pete's? We've got a date to have dinner there one night."

"That'll be a change for him from palace life!" Toby said.

"Back to where we started," Jane remarked. "How are we ever going to get used to life outside the palace, now that we've had a taste of the royal way?"

"We always thought you *did* live a palace life," Toby reminded her.

"Oh, a bit, I suppose. But Boston is not the real thing. Don't tell Armand I said that! Anyway, I think my favorite part of *that* palace was Fenster."

"He was special, wasn't he?" Andy remarked, remembering how nothing ever seemed beyond Fenster. Whatever they needed, he provided.

"We should import him to Baker House," Jane suggested.

"We can take that up with P.A. on our return," Andy said.

"Speaking of P.A.," Toby said, ominously.

Both of her friends looked at her. They knew what she was about to say and they didn't much like it. They'd had all the fun of attending a royal wedding. Now they were going to have to pay the piper: Ms. Allardyce.

"Oh, yes, the paper on Monarchy in the Modern World," Jane said with a sigh. "At least I did a lot of research before we came — you know, for Allegra's queening lessons. We should be able to use that material, don't you think?"

"Not really," Andy said, propping her feet up on the seat across from hers, next to Jane. "After all, every time we tried to use any of the stuff — swamp draining, and what have you — with Allegra, she just pooh-poohed it. I don't think that's what monarchy is about these days."

"So what *is* it about?" Jane challenged.

"Well, according to Allegra, the most important part of monarchy today is friendship and loyalty. At least that's what she wanted to learn about from us."

"You think P.A. wants a paper about friendship and loyalty?" Toby asked.

"If that's what we learned, then I think we owe it to Ms. Allardyce and ourselves to say so," Andy said.

"Maybe," Jane said. "But look at it another way. If friendship and loyalty are what a monarchy is about, then it's pretty clear to me that Canby Hall is a monarchy!"

"And if Canby Hall is a monarchy, P.A. must be the queen — " Toby mused.

"Well that fits," Andy said, cutting her off. "Who is more queenly than P.A.?"

"Well, if Ms. Allardyce is the queen, what does that make us?" Jane asked.

"We're the peasants!" Toby supplied.

Jane looked at Toby oddly. Jane never thought of herself as a peasant. It was a new way of looking at the world.

"Perhaps," she said cautiously. "But one thing is certain. If Canby Hall is a monarchy, and P.A. is the queen, then it's clear that the commoners have all the fun. After all, who needs Fenster, when we've got us?"

"To us!" Andy proposed a toast with her imaginary champagne glass. The girls raised their hands together in triumph.

Who is Andy's secret admirer? Jane and Toby try to figure it out. Read The Girls of Canby Hall #32, WHO HAS A CRUSH ON ANDY?

The Girls of Canby Hall®

by Emily Chase

School pressures! Boy trouble! Roommate rivalry! The girls of Canby Hall are learning about life and love now that they've left home to live in a private boarding school.

Complete series available wherever you buy books.